# Hoop Crazy!

ORCA
YOUNG
READERS

# Hoop Crazy!

## ERIC WALTERS

ORCA BOOK PUBLISHERS

**Library and Archives Canada Cataloguing in Publication**

Walters, Eric, 1957–

Hoop crazy!

ISBN 10: 1-55143-184-X / ISBN 13: 978-1-55143-184-0

I. Title.
PS8595.A598H66 2001   jC813'.54   C2001-910202-X
PZ7.W17129Ho 2001

First published in the United States, 2001
**Library of Congress Control Number**: 2001087478

**Summary**: A new coach teaches Nick and Kia about courage and leadership.

Orca Book Publishers gratefully acknowledges the support for its publishing
programs provided by the following agencies: the Government of Canada through
the Book Publishing Industry Development Program and the Canada Council for the
Arts, and the Province of British Columbia through the BC Arts Council
and the Book Publishing Tax Credit.

Cover design by Teresa Bubela
Interior illustrations by John Mantha

ORCA BOOK PUBLISHERS
PO Box 5626, STN. B
VICTORIA, BC CANADA
V8R 6S4

ORCA BOOK PUBLISHERS
PO Box 468
CUSTER, WA USA
98240-0468

www.orcabook.com
Printed and bound in Canada.

11 10 09 08 • 7 6 5 4

*This book is dedicated to Al Alilovic, Jordan Henry, Mark Pupavac and Nick Walters: four young men who made it all the way to the semifinals of the NBA-sponsored three-on-three tournament in Toronto and let me come along to watch.*

# Chapter One

"What do you mean you can't play!" I barked into the phone.

"It's not my fault, Nick!" Jordan pleaded. "My father just sprung it on us last night."

"Sprung what on you?"

"We're going on vacation. He's being sent away on a business trip and the whole family is going."

"When do you leave?"

"On Friday. We'll be gone for two weeks."

"Can't you just tell your parents you don't want to go?" I asked.

"I told them. They said I had no choice."

"Can you come back for a couple of days in the middle so you could still be on our team for the contest?"

"Can't do that. We're going to Europe."

"Europe!" I exclaimed.

"We're going to see eleven countries in twelve days. Do you know what that means?" Jordan asked.

"Besides the fact you won't be here to be part of our three-on-three team?"

"Besides that. It means I'm going to see museums and art galleries and historical stuff in more countries than I have fingers or toes."

"That doesn't sound too exciting," I admitted.

"Can you spell boring? It's going to be awful."

"Maybe your parents will let you do some fun stuff," I offered.

"Doubtful."

"Why do parents love boring old stuff so much?" I asked.

"I don't know, but my parents just love museums."

"Maybe it's because it reminds them of when they were young," I suggested.

"Maybe. I'm really sorry about bailing out on everybody, but it's not my fault."

"I know, I know."

"And I'd much rather be staying here and playing basketball," Jordan added.

"Who wouldn't?"

"And there's still the three of you. I'm sure you can find a fourth person to replace me."

"A fourth person is easy to find. Replacing you isn't," I said.

Jordan was our "big man." He was tall and had long

arms and springs in his legs, and shoes that were only one size smaller than my father's. Imagine that, a kid going into grade four who wore size nine sneakers. It really would be hard to have somebody "fill his shoes" for this tournament.

"You want me to send you a postcard or two?" Jordan asked.

"That would be nice."

"Of course you have to realize that whatever I send will have a picture of a museum or art gallery on it," he said forlornly.

"That's okay...I guess."

"I'll call you as soon as I get back. You'll do well. Bye."

"Sure, take care," I said as I put down the phone and left the family room. Maybe something to eat would make me feel better.

Poor Jordan, having to see a bunch of old and dead things with his parents instead of staying here and hanging around with his friends and playing in a basketball tournament.

We'd been talking about the tournament for months— Kia, Mark, Jordan and me. It was a special three-on-three tournament and was sponsored by the NBA. It was held in cities across North America throughout the summer and it was coming to our city—our city! There would be hundreds and hundreds of teams of different ages and we'd be part of it—at least we *were* going to be part of it.

"Darn!" I said as I kicked the side of the fridge.

"Hey, easy on the appliances," my father said as he put down the newspaper he was reading at the kitchen table.

"Sorry," I mumbled.

"You don't want to get that fridge mad at you or it may stop feeding you. So what are you so upset about?"

"Jordan isn't going to be part of our team."

"That's serious. What happened?"

"Family vacation…Europe…can't get out of it."

"Stuff happens. You'll have to find another player," he said.

"I know what I have to do. Doing it is harder. Everybody we know is already gone, going, busy, or they suck."

"That is a problem," my father said.

"What's a problem?" my mother asked as she came into the kitchen.

"Jordan can't play with us in the tournament so we have to find another—"

"Basketball," she said with disgust, cutting me off. "I don't want to hear another word about basketball!"

"But you don't understand," I protested.

"I understand. What you don't understand is how sick I am of basketball."

"How can you ever get sick of basketball?" I asked.

"Easy. When you first started playing when you were little, it was just in the winter. And then it started to be a game you played in the fall and winter."

I guess she had a point. Besides playing pick-up ball on the driveway, Kia and I were on the same rep team, and we'd been on the school team, and we'd even been part of the winning three-on-three team in a contest at school.

"It seemed like the year had only two seasons—basketball and summer," my mother continued. "At least we had the summer free...but now? It's summer so there shouldn't be any basketball."

"Come on, Mom, it's not like it's the whole summer. It's just one day," I argued.

"The tournament is just one day long. The planning and the practice and the discussions never seem to end! So now do you understand why I don't want to hear about it?"

"We understand," my father said softly.

"Sure," I said, shrugging my shoulders.

"Good. Now here we are together on a wonderful, warm Wednesday evening. How about if the three of us go for a bicycle ride?" she asked cheerfully.

"Not me," I said. "I've got to make some phone calls and try and find a fourth player for our team for the—"

My mother shrieked, threw her arms up into the

air, and ran from the room. My father and I exchanged a look.

"She took that better than I thought she might have," my father said. "You make those phone calls and I'll go and talk to your mother."

"I didn't mean to get her upset."

"She'll get over it." He smiled. "Maybe I'll even offer to go on a little bike ride with her."

# Chapter Two

My first phone call had been to Kia. After I finally convinced her that I wasn't joking around about Jordan leaving, she came straight over to my house and we started to make phone calls.

The phone started to ring. One…two…three…

"Hello."

"Hi, this is Nick. Can I speak to Tyler?"

"Sorry, he's not here," said a woman. I was pretty sure it was his mother. "He's away at camp."

"Will he be home soon?"

"Two weeks tomorrow."

That was no good. "Okay, thanks…good-bye," I said as I hung up the phone.

"Any luck?" Kia asked.

"Lots. All bad."

We'd already made more then a dozen phone calls.

Most of the people I'd talked to, but with three I left messages on their answering machines. Maybe one of those people would call back. That was our only hope.

"Any other ideas who I should call?"

"We've tried everybody I can think of," Kia said. "People are all either out, away on vacation, already committed to something or just not interested."

"Maybe somebody will return one of the messages we left," I said hopefully.

"That would be nice." She paused. "I'd at least like to hear from Mark."

Mark was the third member of our team. I'd called him just after I called Kia. He wasn't home, so I'd left a message on his machine.

"Well, somebody has to call us, and they have to call us soon."

It did have to be soon. The application for the tournament had to be completed and handed in by six o'clock today. All our names and information had been filled in. I'd used White Out to cover Jordan's part of the application. All I needed now was a new name to take his place.

"I was thinking," Kia said. "The rules do say we have to have four people, right?"

"Yep. It's clear. Each three-on-three team must be composed of four players."

"But does it say anything about how much each player has to play?"

"I don't think so," I said. I'd gone over those rules pretty closely.

"So, technically you could leave the same three players on the court the whole game and the other player could stay on the bench."

"Yeah, I guess so. Three players could play the whole game."

"Which means that you and me and Mark could play all the time," Kia said.

"We can't even enter without a fourth name," I said. "That's the rules."

"I know that, but if we had a fourth person he wouldn't even need to play…right?"

"Yeah, but that wouldn't be very much fun for the fourth guy, and not particularly fair."

"Okay, then maybe we could let him play a little bit, or when we're really, really ahead," Kia suggested.

"That would be better," I agreed.

"And because of that we don't necessarily need a good fourth player," she said.

"You're right. All we really need is a body."

"*Any* body," she said.

"Like Kevin," I said. Kevin lived three doors down. He wasn't the best basketball player—actually he was terrible—but he was a good guy and played with us all the time on the driveway. He never complained, even when he was getting hammered.

"Do you want to call or should I?" I asked.

"Um…you should."

I picked up the phone and dialed his number. It started to ring.

"Hello."

"Hi, Kev, it's Nick. How are you doing?"

"Good. And you?"

"Not so good. We've lost Jordan and we're looking for a fourth player for our three-on-three team."

There was a pause. I guess he couldn't believe I was asking him.

"And you want me?"

"Yeah. Do you think you want to play?"

There was another long pause. "No, thank you," he said coolly.

"But why not?" I asked.

"Ask Kia. Talk to you later," he said as he hung up.

I put the phone down and turned to Kia.

"Did he say no?" Kia asked.

I nodded my head. "And he said that you'd know why he said no."

"Me? How would I know?" Kia said, looking away.

"You are the worst liar I've ever met!" I exclaimed.

"Well you're not much better," she said.

"Fine, good, so neither one of us can lie very well. Now tell me why Kevin won't play with us?"

"I told him he couldn't," she said quietly.

"When did you do that?" I asked.

"A couple of months ago. You know, when we started talking about forming a team and Kevin asked if he could maybe be on our team."

"So you told him he couldn't?"

She nodded her head, but still wasn't looking at me.

"What else did you say to him, Kia?"

"I sort of told him he could be on our team...if he was the last player left in the entire city."

"Nice. Very nice. And now that we need him, we—"

The phone rang. Maybe it was somebody calling us back! I grabbed the phone.

"Hello!"

"Hello, is this Nicholas?" a woman asked.

"Yes, this is Nick."

"It's so good to talk to you. Do you know who this is?"

"No," I admitted, although I knew who it wasn't—somebody calling back to say they would be on our team.

"This is Debbie...your mother's cousin Debbie."

"Oh, hi."

"Is your mother there? I have some great news to share!" she chirped cheerfully.

"I'll go and get her."

I put down the phone and went to look for her.

"Mom! Telephone!" I screamed.

"There's no need to yell. I'm right here," she said.

"Sorry. Telephone for you."

"Do you know who it is?" she asked.

"Your cousin Debbie."

"My cousin?"

"That's what she said."

"Oh my goodness!" she gasped as she started to run out of the room toward the phone.

I trailed after her, catching up just as she picked up the phone.

"Mom," I called out. "Do you think you could keep it short? We're waiting for some calls about basketball."

Her mouth dropped open and then her eyes came to life, burning a hole right through me, and I knew I really, really shouldn't have said that.

"That's okay," I stammered. "Take as long as you want."

"We're going to go now...to the kitchen...to eat... and leave you alone," I stammered as I grabbed Kia and pulled her to her feet and dragged her out the door.

"What was that all about?" Kia asked.

"I thought we should let my mother have some privacy on the phone. Are you hungry?"

"I'm always hungry. Got any cookies?"

"Lots. You know where they are," I said.

Kia went to the cupboard and pulled out a big bag of cookies. She knew her way around my house as well as I did...maybe better. She was my best friend and we practically lived at each other's houses. I went to the fridge and pulled out the milk, grabbed two glasses and poured us both a drink.

"These are good," Kia mumbled through a mouthful of cookies.

I stuffed in a couple of cookies, chewed and washed them down with a gulp of milk.

"Is your mother off the phone yet?" Kia asked.

Almost on cue my mother came into the kitchen.

"I have wonderful news!" she said.

I almost asked if she'd found somebody to be on our team, but thought better of it.

"What news?" Kia asked.

"My cousin Debbie and her son Ned are coming to visit! They'll be arriving on Monday and they're going to be in town for a whole week! Isn't that wonderful!"

"Yeah, great," I said, unable to even fake enthusiasm.

"Her husband has a conference to attend. And while he's at the conference, they'll be staying with us!"

"Here? In our house?"

"Of course here. Debbie will use the guest room and Ned will share your room."

"Who's Ned?" Kia asked.

"Debbie's son. He's exactly the same age as you and Nick," my mother answered.

"Our age?"

"He was actually born on the same day as Nick.

April twenty-third. His mother and I were always the closest cousins and then we had our sons on the same day. Isn't that amazing!"

"Yeah, amazing," Kia agreed. "Imagine that, somebody the same age as us is going to be staying here for a week."

Instantly I knew what Kia was getting at—Ned could be our fourth player. She didn't know Ned or she'd know that idea was crazy.

"By the way, does Ned play basketball?" Kia asked.

"I don't know if—"

"No, he doesn't play," I said, cutting off my mother.

"And how would you know that?" my mother asked.

"Because he's Ned the Nerd. He doesn't play basketball, or soccer, or hockey, or any sports. He doesn't do *anything* normal."

"You can't say that," my mother said. "You haven't seen him for years."

"And those have been good years."

"Don't be that way, Nick," my mother said. She turned to Kia. "When Nick and Ned were little, our two families used to spend time together every summer on vacation. They were wonderful vacations!"

"Wonderful for you maybe. You didn't have to play with Nerd."

"Please don't call him that."

14

"Fine. You didn't have to spend time with Ned. He's strange."

"Like how?" Kia asked.

"Like he's always using these big words and he has really thick glasses—"

"That's not his fault," my mother said. "And it isn't nice to make fun of people for things like that."

"Fine. And he's crazy about bugs. Just crazy. He wants to be some sort of bug guy when he grows up."

"You mean like Spiderman?" Kia asked.

"No, not like that. Like a guy who knows all about bugs. There's a name for it."

"An entomologist."

"Whatever."

"And you don't know if that's what he still wants to be. It's been over three years since we've seen them. He could be different."

"He was always *different*."

"I mean he could have changed."

"Not from what you read to me from the letters your cousin sends," I said. "He still sounds weird."

"How come you stopped going on vacation with them?" Kia asked.

"Debbie's husband is a forest ranger."

"You mean like in Yogi the Bear cartoons?" Kia questioned.

"Like a real forest ranger and they were transferred across the country to a very remote forest in a national park," my mother explained. "And since summer is the busiest time of the year for forest rangers, they can't readily take time off when we usually take our vacation."

"So why are they coming now?" I asked.

"Debbie's husband is presenting at some sort of conference just north of here. And since he's going to be so busy there, I suggested that Debbie and Ned spend the time here with us."

"Lucky us."

"And while I spend time catching up with Debbie, you'll have lots of time to spend with Ned."

"Great...just great."

"You just have to play with him."

"I don't have time to play. We have the three-on-three tournament during that time and we have to practice and we still have to find a fourth player and—"

"You still haven't found anybody?" my mother asked.

"Not yet. We have a few possibilities."

"What about Ned?" my mother asked. "That would be perfect."

"That would be perfectly awful. I'm telling you he can't play basketball!" I protested. "There's no way I want him on my—"

"Yes, we do!" Kia said, cutting me off.

"No, we don't!"

"Yes, we do," Kia said, staring at me. "Look at the time, Nick."

I knew what she was getting at. We really didn't have much time left.

Kia turned to my mother. "Could you please call your cousin back and see if her son wants to be on our team."

"Nick?" my mother asked. "Is that okay?"

"Sure, whatever," I mumbled.

My mother burst into a smile. "I'll call Debbie back right now and ask her about Ned being on your team."

"Great!" Kia said and my mother rushed out of the room to make the phone call.

"That was a mistake," I said.

"At least this way we have a team."

# Chapter Three

"You don't know Nerd," I hissed at Kia.

"I don't need to know him. All I need to know is that he's human, our age and can be the fourth member of our team."

"But I don't want him on our team."

"It's either him or we don't have a team," Kia said.

"But he can't play basketball."

"That's perfect."

"How can that be perfect?"

"If he doesn't play, then he won't mind being on the bench so much."

"But he can't play at all!"

"All he has to do is be able to sit on a bench. He can do that, can't he?"

"With Nerd I'm not too sure. He'd probably miss the bench and—"

"Great news!"

I seriously doubted it.

"Ned will be on your team! Isn't that great!"

"Yeah, great," I mumbled.

"His mother said he doesn't know much about basketball, but she thinks it would be good for him."

"Good for him?" Kia questioned. "What does that mean?"

"Well…I think he doesn't play many sports."

"Try no sports," I said.

"Debbie said he's still rather tall—"

"How tall is he?" Kia asked.

My mother shook her head. "I don't really know…I didn't ask. But she said that because he's always been tall for his age she always thought he could be a good player."

"It's about more than being tall," I said.

"But height does matter," my mother said.

"If that was all that did matter they'd just line us up before the game, measure all the players and give the game to the tallest team."

My mother shot me a dirty look and I knew it was probably wise to shut up at that point.

"Debbie said that Ned is a very fast study. She thought with the proper teachers he could become quite good, and I told her we had two excellent teachers for him."

"Three. There's Mark too," Kia said. "He's about the best outside shooter I know."

"He's such a nice boy…very polite…never a problem to have around the house," my mother said. "Is he always that quiet?"

"Not always," I said, although he was one of the quietest people I knew. "He's the best outside shooter of anybody."

"Even better, so Ned will have three teachers. I got all the information from Debbie and I'll fill in Ned's spot on the form," my mother said, holding it out for me to see. "When does this have to be handed in?"

I looked at my watch. "In three hours."

"That's cutting it a little close, isn't it?" she asked.

I shrugged. "This isn't the way we planned it."

"I'll drop it off on my way to get groceries."

"That would be great," Kia said.

"Yeah, thanks."

"It sounds like you were lucky that I could get Debbie. She was just getting ready to drive away to her house when I called and they got her," my mother said.

"Couldn't you have just called her at home?" Kia asked.

"They don't have a phone."

"They don't have a phone?" Kia repeated, not believing her ears. "Why don't they have a phone?"

"It's not that they don't want one, it's that they can't have one. There are no phone lines where they live."

"Come on, there are phone lines everywhere," Kia said.

"Not deep in the bush."

"What about a cell phone?" she asked.

"Too far out. No reception. They're over a three-hour drive from the nearest town. Even their closest neighbor is more than thirty minutes away."

"Why would anybody live that far away from everything?" Kia asked.

"They don't have any choice in their line of work. You can't be a forest ranger and live in the middle of the city."

"But if they're that far away from everybody, where does Ned go to school?" Kia asked.

"He doesn't," I answered.

"Now there's a bonus. No school."

"He has school," my mother said. "He just doesn't go out for it."

Kia looked confused. "You mean the school comes to him?"

"Not exactly. The lessons come to him. He takes school by correspondence."

"By mail," I said, not knowing if Kia knew what correspondence meant.

"He gets lessons mailed to him, he fills them out, sends them back to be marked, and then they send him the next lessons," my mother explained.

"That's awful," Kia said. "He still has to do all the work, but he doesn't get to talk to friends, or play games, or have gym classes or anything."

"He only gets the bad parts," I agreed.

"His mother is quite proud of him. Apparently he's working well above his grade level," my mother said.

"That's no surprise," I said. "What else does he have to do except study?"

"Who does he hang around with?" Kia asked.

"He spends a great deal of time with his parents."

"No, that isn't what I mean," she said. "Are there kids for him to spend time with...to play with?"

My mother shook her head. "As I said, the nearest neighbor is pretty far away, and as I recall from one of Debbie's letters, they don't have any children."

"I'd hate having no other kids to hang with," Kia said.

"It would be hard. Debbie told me that even though they haven't seen each other in three years, Ned still considers Nick to be one of his best friends."

"Me?" I asked in shock.

"She said he still talks about the times you two spent together and all the fun you had."

"I remember the times, I just don't remember the fun."

What I did remember was Ned always using big words and talking about things I didn't understand and didn't want to know about.

"You had lots of fun together," my mother said. "Hold on, I know what will refresh your memory. I'll go and get the photo albums!"

"Mom, please don't get the..."

She was gone before I could finish the sentence.

"Don't worry," Kia said.

"Worry about what?"

"About me getting in the way of you and your best friend Ned. I'll just come around to play a little basketball and then I'll leave so you and Ned can have fun together!" Kia teased.

"I have a better idea. Maybe *I* should leave *before* he gets here."

"Here they are," my mother said, re-entering the kitchen with a stack of albums. "There'll be some pictures in a whole lot of different albums, so we'll just have to browse through them all."

"Come on, Mom, I really don't want to look at old pictures."

"I do," Kia said. "I love photo albums."

"So do I," my mother agreed.

I knew there was hardly any point in arguing with one of them, so fighting two of them was definitely a losing battle.

"Now I'm pretty sure this is the album that contains the last vacation we spent together," my mother said as she started flipping through the pages. "Here, here they are!"

Kia and I looked over her shoulder at the pictures. There was a whole page.

"Here's one!" she said, pointing with her finger.

It was a picture of Ned and me standing together. I was dressed in a T-shirt and cutoff shorts. He wore long pants and had on a long-sleeved shirt and a big goofy hat. He was "allergic" to the sun. I was holding a baseball bat and he held a large butterfly net.

"One of you is pretty confused about what you were doing," Kia said.

"No confusion on my part," I said. "Dad suggested we catch a few flies and Ned went to get his net instead of a glove because he didn't know what Dad meant by "flies'."

Kia started to chuckle.

"I'm glad you find it funny."

"It is," my mother said.

"It wasn't. All he wanted to do was collect bugs, or read about bugs, or talk about bugs and—"

"Sounds like you and basketball," my mother said, cutting me off.

"That's different!"

"How?" she asked.

"For one thing, it's basketball."

"He is tall, isn't he," Kia said, looking down at the picture.

I looked down. He did have that going for him. He was almost a full head taller than me.

"That was our last vacation together. These pictures were taken almost four years ago. I know I have lots of earlier ones," my mother said.

She grabbed another album and started to flip through the pages.

"Anybody thirsty?" my mother asked.

"I am," Kia said.

"Me too."

"Good. Nick, get us all a drink will you?" my mother asked.

I was going to argue, but getting people a drink was better than the alternative—looking at pictures.

I grabbed three glasses and put them down on the table. Next I pulled out a big container of lemonade. Kia didn't like lemonade that much, but I did, and if she wanted something else she could get it herself.

"Oh, look at this one!" my mother exclaimed. "This is one of Nick and Ned when they were about one year old. Aren't they adorable!" she cooed.

My mother thought every picture of me was adorable—that was part of a mother's job.

"That is a great shot," Kia agreed. "And they both fit into that bathtub so well."

"Bathtub!" I gasped, choking on my lemonade as it started to go down the wrong way.

"Yes, when you two were little, you shared a bath a lot of nights."

"That's so cute!" Kia said.

"Let me have a look at that!" I demanded, grabbing the album and practically ripping it out of their hands.

It was a picture of Ned and me—little babies—sitting in a little plastic bathtub, having a bubble bath. We were both smiling and I was holding a small, yellow rubber duckie.

"You *must* be good friends to be sharing a bath," Kia said.

I didn't know what bothered me more, Kia seeing the picture or my mother thinking it was okay for anybody to see the picture. Thank goodness it was a bubble bath and the suds filled up the whole bottom of the picture, blocking other things from view, or this could have been really embarrassing.

"I've got to get going to drop off the contest application," my mother said. "Do you want me to put away the albums or do you two want to look at the pictures some more?"

"Put them away!" I said. "Far away."

"Aaahhh, couldn't we look at them some more?" Kia said. "Are there any more pictures of baby Nicky?"

"Oh sure, we have albums and albums of them," my mother said.

"We don't have time for that," I said. "We have to practice our plays."

"Maybe another time," my mother said.

"Maybe," Kia agreed.

Over my dead body, I thought, but I didn't say anything.

# Chapter Four

I drove the ball deep while Kia broke back setting up a screen to knock off the "invisible man" who was covering Mark. He brushed by her and set up just on the edge of the three-point line. I threw out a pass and he quickly put it up—rim, backboard and then into the net.

"Nice shot," I said.

Mark nodded, but didn't answer.

"Let's do it again," I said.

Everybody got back into position.

When Jordan left to go away on vacation he took with him three weeks' worth of plans and plays. Because he was so strong down low in the post we'd built most of our plays around him. Now, without somebody big, we had to rely more on Mark and his outside shooting. That was what we'd been working on for the past two days.

I passed the ball out to Mark as he came off the screen Kia had set. He put the ball up and it dropped in. Thank goodness Mark was so reliable.

"Let's take a break," Kia said.

"A short break," I offered.

The three of us plopped down on the grass in the shade at the edge of the driveway.

"We've worked hard today," Kia said.

"And we have to keep on working hard for the next five days."

"When are Ned and his mother supposed to arrive?" Kia asked.

"Today some time."

"You really aren't looking forward to this, are you?" she asked.

"Not particularly. You don't know this guy. He's always bragging about how much stuff he knows, and he uses really big words—I think he does that just to show how smart he thinks he is—and all he wants to talk about are stupid things."

"I don't even know the guy and I already don't like him," Kia said.

"Maybe he's changed," Mark said.

"Mark's right," she agreed. "You haven't seen him for years. Maybe he's got new interests. Maybe he's even fun to be around."

"I doubt that very much."

"You never can tell. People change…right, Mark?"

Mark nodded his head.

"But sometimes they stay the same," I said. "Right, Mark?"

Mark shrugged his shoulders. "Sometimes."

I was about to say something else when my attention was caught by the sight of a big, dirty, four-wheel-drive vehicle, slowly moving down the otherwise deserted street. It pulled over to the curb and came to a stop right in front of my house.

"Is that them?" Kia asked.

"I don't know, but it looks like what a forest ranger would drive," I said.

The door opened and a woman climbed out. I hadn't seen her for years, but I recognized her—maybe more from the pictures we'd been looking at than from my memory. It was my mother's cousin Debbie. She had flaming red hair that hung down her back. It was so bright I wondered if it would glow in the dark.

"Hello!" she called, waving a hand over her head.

I waved back. "Kia, could you go and let my mother know they're here."

"I'll go," Mark offered.

"Thanks."

As Mark went off to get my mother, Kia and I headed to the car.

"Hello, Nicholas!" she said as she reached out, grabbed me and gave me a hug, practically pulling me off my feet.

"Hi," I managed to answer back.

"You're so big! You've grown so much!" she beamed as she released me.

"A little bit," I mumbled. "Um, this is my friend Kia."

"Pleased to meet you, Kia," she said.

"Me too. So where's your son?" Kia asked.

"Oh," she said. "He's right here."

She turned around and opened up the back door. There was Ned. He was holding a book in his hand, thick glasses on his face, frizzy red hair sticking up in the air in twenty different directions. He did look tall.

"Come on out, Ned," she said.

He put down the book, looked at us like he not only didn't know who we were, but where he was. And then he started to climb out of the truck. He kept coming and coming and coming until he stood there towering over me! I looked up in total shock. He was like a giant.

"Ned's grown a little too," his mother said.

"A little?" Kia gasped. "He's…he's…he's—"

"Tall for his age," his mother said, cutting her off.

"He's tall for any age," Kia answered. "How tall are you?"

"I'm five foot eight inches tall," Ned said.

"And you're only going into grade four?" Kia questioned.

"No, I'm going into grade six."

"But I thought you and Nick were born on the same day?" Kia asked.

"We were. I'm *supposed* to be going into grade four, but I'm so smart I'm going into grade six."

His tone of voice was a combination of bragging and whining, which together had the same quality as fingernails running down a blackboard.

"I don't feel so well," Ned said.

"I told you not to read in the car so much. It always affects your stomach," his mother replied.

"I feel like I'm going to…going to…"

Kia and I jumped backward as Ned vomited all over the driveway.

"That was close!" Kia exclaimed.

"Too close. Look at your shoes," I said in disgust. Both of our basketball shoes had gotten sprayed!

"That's disgusting…just disgusting," Kia gagged.

***

"That certainly was special," I said as I finished hosing down the driveway. I'd already done our shoes and they were sitting in a sunny spot on the porch, drying off.

"You'll never forget Ned's arrival. That's for sure," Kia giggled.

"I'm glad you think it was funny."

"Not really, but it *could* have been funny," she said.

"How?"

"If he'd only got your shoes," she chuckled. "It reminded me of one of those disaster movies. It was like a volcano erupting."

"I guess that's a matter of opinion. That was typical Nerd behavior."

"You mean he's vomited on you before?" Kia asked.

"No, but he's always doing something like that. Getting sick, or having an allergic reaction, or getting bitten by bugs, or tripping and hurting himself."

"I couldn't believe it. I'm just glad it was only our shoes."

"It was close," I said.

"He must feel embarrassed."

"I don't care what he feels," I said.

"Do you think he'll be up to practicing today?" Kia asked.

"Practicing…like in basketball?"

She nodded her head. "I was thinking that maybe we could run a few plays with him. He's even taller than Jordan."

"So is my house, and some of these trees, but they can't run plays either," I said. "No matter how tall he is, he's still Nerd."

"What harm would it do to just try a few plays with him?"

"It wouldn't do any harm, it just wouldn't do any good," I argued. "Besides, I have to go in and entertain our guests and have dinner. Do you want to stay?"

"Not me. My family is going out for dinner."

"Too bad. Are you sure you can't stay?"

"Family obligation. Besides, I wouldn't want to interfere...you know...come between you and your old best friend."

"Come on, Kia, you know he's not my best friend."

She smiled. "I know that," she said. "And you know that. But from what your mother said, I don't think Ned knows that. See you later."

\*\*\*

"Could you pass the potatoes, please," Debbie asked, and the serving bowl was passed down the table to her.

"Are these organically grown?" she asked as she hesitated, spoon in hand, before putting any of them on her plate.

"I really don't know," my mother said apologetically. "Probably not."

"I guess I can still have some," Debbie said. "Although Ned you should be careful. We don't want your allergies acting up."

"He's allergic to potatoes?" I asked in amazement.

"Not to potatoes, but to the things that they put on potatoes," she said.

"You mean like butter and sour cream?"

Everybody at the table started to laugh.

"I think she means the chemicals or pesticides," my mother said.

"I'm afraid that doesn't leave much that you can eat," my father said.

"I'm so sorry," my mother apologized again. "I just didn't know that your family had all become vegetarians."

"We're just trying to eat well," Debbie said.

"Same with me," added my father.

He not only had his steak, but he'd had Mom cook up the one that Debbie hadn't wanted. He looked quite pleased with himself as he continued to cut up one of his steaks. I guess I couldn't say much myself—I had the steak that would have been Ned's.

"So Ned, you're going to be playing with Nick and his friends in the tournament," my father said.

"I guess so."

"Do you play much basketball?"

"Not really."

"Do you have a hoop on your driveway?" my father asked.

"No," Ned said.

"We don't really have a driveway," Debbie said. "It's more like a rutted place where we park the Rover."

"So that just leaves playing at school," my father said.

"Ned doesn't go to school," I said.

"He's homeschooled," his mother added.

"That's right, I remember hearing something about

that," my father said between chews. "So where do you play basketball?"

"I guess I don't."

There was a pause as everybody digested that fact.

"Ever?" my father asked, breaking the silence.

"A couple of times when we were in town shopping. There's a basket up in the playground."

"That's good," my father said. "Don't worry, it's a simple game. Right, Nick?"

"Sure."

"And as long as you're prepared to work hard over the next few days you'll learn a lot. Are you going to practice every day this week, Nick?"

"Of course."

"Every day?" Ned asked.

"Sure…why, did you have something else planned?" I asked.

"I was hoping to get down to the Museum of Natural History or maybe the planetarium," Ned said.

This guy was truly unbelievable. Unfortunately it was too late and Jordan and his family had already left for Europe or maybe I could have worked out a deal—Ned could go with Jordan's family to see the museums of Europe and Jordan could stay here and play ball. That way everybody would have been happy.

I opened my mouth to say something when I caught sight of the look my mother was throwing me. I closed my mouth.

"There'll be time for everything, I'm sure," my mother said. "The museum is open until nine o'clock tonight. Maybe we could all go. Wouldn't that be fun?"

"That would be wonderful!" Debbie exclaimed.

"I'd like that a lot," Ned said.

"I'm afraid I'll have to pass," my father said. "I've got some work to do that I just have to finish off before tomorrow."

"That's too bad," my mother said.

The tone of her voice left little doubt that she didn't believe my father any more than I did. He just didn't want to go. Neither did I.

"Then there'll just be the *four* of us," she continued, fixing me with her gaze.

It didn't take much mathematics to know what that meant—the two of them, my mother and me.

"Won't that be fun, Nick?" my mother said, although I knew she wasn't so much asking me as telling me.

"Sure," I said, nodding my head. It would probably be just about the most "fun" thing I'd do with Nerd.

# Chapter Five

"So where should we go first?" Debbie asked.

I was thinking either the exit, the gift shop or the snack bar, but I was smart enough to stay quiet. My mother had already warned me about making "snarky" little remarks to Nerd. It was hard. He was annoying. Really annoying.

"I'd like to go to see the dinosaur exhibit," Ned said.

"You like dinosaurs?" I asked. I thought he only liked bugs.

"Don't you?" he asked.

"They're okay…if you're in grade one."

My mother shot me another dirty look and I buttoned my lip.

"They have one of the best Cretaceous era collections in the world," Ned said. "Let's go straight there."

"I thought you wanted to see the dinosaurs?" I questioned.

"That is the dinosaurs," Ned said with a chuckle. "Don't you know *anything* about dinosaurs?"

"I know that I think they're—" I stopped myself as I caught sight of the look my mother was giving me.

"Didn't you do a project on dinosaurs in school, Nick?" she asked.

"Yep. Grade one."

She shot me another one of those don't-you-dare looks.

"And that's when I learned how interesting they are," I said.

I trudged along behind my mother, Debbie and Nerd. He was trying to read a museum guidebook as we walked, giving out directions and little tidbits of information, most of which I didn't understand...or care to understand.

"They also have a very complete set of amber holding various specimens of insect life," Ned gushed.

"Bugs?"

"Insects in amber...trapped from prehistoric times. Isn't that excellent!"

"Yeah. Almost as exciting as the dinosaurs," I mumbled.

"So first we'll see the dinosaurs and then—excuse me!" Ned said loudly as he bumped into a woman pushing a stroller.

"I'm so sorry…I was reading and I didn't see you."

"That's alright, nobody was hurt," the woman said.

"I was just excited to go and see the dinosaurs," Ned explained.

"It's a great collection. Especially those from the Cretaceous era."

Did everybody in the world except me know about this?

"I'm sure you and your brother will enjoy it," she said.

"He's not my brother!" I protested.

Ned shook his head. "We're good friends. We were even born on the same day."

"The same day in the same year?" she asked.

Ned nodded his head. "We're the same age exactly."

"Not exactly," Debbie said. "Nick was born three hours before you, Ned, so he's older than you."

"That's hard to believe," the woman said, using a tone like she really didn't believe it.

"I'm the right size for my age," I said. "It's him that's different."

"He certainly is—"

She stopped as her baby, who had been gurgling, started to cry.

"Enjoy the dinosaurs, boys," she said, "and I'll take care of my own little monster."

We started off again.

"That happens to Ned all the time," Debbie said.

"You mean bumping into things?" I asked.

"I meant people always thinking he's older. Although you're right, he is always bumping into something."

"That was a some*one*," I corrected her.

"That's not usually a problem where we live," she said with a laugh. "But it would be more of an issue here. There are always so many people around."

"Here?" I asked. The museum was practically deserted.

"Everywhere," Debbie said. "At home it's not unusual for us to go two or three weeks at a time without seeing anybody but each other."

"That would certainly be different," my mother agreed. "I'm not sure I could get used to that."

"I'm sure that I couldn't," I said. "I like having people around."

"Here it is!" Ned exclaimed.

We were standing before a narrow passage. I recognized it as being the entrance to the dinosaur hall. The lighting was low and the walls were covered with fake bamboo and painted with pictures of dinosaurs. We walked along, the sound of drumming coming from hidden speakers. That was so stupid—like who did they think was doing the drumming back then?

The passage opened up to the dinosaur hall. It was gigantic, with a high, high ceiling. All around us were the massive remains of the dinosaurs. They were gigantic!

I stopped and looked up and stared. It took my breath away. It had been years since I'd been here—since grade one—and I'd forgotten how big and impressive this was. It was my favorite place in the whole museum.

"Pretty amazing, isn't it?" my mother said.

"It's really…" I stopped myself. "Okay."

"Just okay?" Debbie asked.

"Maybe it would be more impressive if you hadn't been here before."

"How long can we stay?" Ned asked.

"We can stay as long as you want," his mother said.

I looked at my watch. Closing time was in two hours. That would be long enough…maybe I could even come back some other time with my mother. Some time when Ned wasn't around to spoil it.

# Chapter Six

"Look, Ned, books are good, but you have to play if you want to understand the game," I said.

"I'm almost finished," he said.

He was sitting on a folding chair on the lawn beside the driveway while Mark and Kia and I played ball. At least if he'd been looking at us, instead of having his nose buried in the book, he might have learned a couple of the plays.

"How about if we take a break for a drink," Kia suggested.

"Sure. A five-minute break would be okay."

I walked into the garage and turned on the tap. By the time I reached the end of the hose, Kia was already through drinking and Mark was slurping down water. I waited for my turn. It was cold and felt wonderful as it slopped into my mouth and down my throat as well as spilling all over my chin and onto my T-shirt. Water from a hose when you were tired and hot was just about the best thing in the world.

"You want a drink?" I called over to Ned.

Ned looked up from the book. "What?" he asked. There was a look of total confusion on his face. I didn't know if that was from my question or what he was reading. Either way I wasn't encouraged.

"Do you want a drink?" I repeated. "Reading can really work up a sweat."

"Um...I'm fine," he mumbled, diving back into the book.

He was reading a book on basketball that he'd found on one of the shelves in my room. It had been around since I was little. It was a pretty good book—written by a former NBA player—but was no substitute for actually having played the game more than two or three times in your life.

"He is awfully tall," Kia said quietly as she stood beside me.

"You're right about both things," I said, lowering my voice and turning away from Ned.

"What do you mean both things?"

"He is tall...and he is awful."

Mark quietly chuckled to himself.

"You don't know that. He could be good."

"You're right...he has almost finished the *entire* book, so he could be just wonderful," I said sarcastically.

"Let me just try," Kia said. "Besides, you told me

your mother wanted you to include him, and if he just sits there all day without playing, you could be in trouble."

She had a point. "Sure, run a few plays. I'll sit out… right here where I can see everything."

I plopped down on the grass—right into a spot where the hose was still running. Instantly I was soaked right through. It felt nice.

"Come on, Ned, it's your turn to play," Kia said.

"I've just got two pages to go," he protested.

Kia grabbed the book from him. "It ends with everybody living happily ever after," she said. "Now get up and play."

Reluctantly he rose to his feet. He just towered over Kia. Somehow I'd almost forgotten just how tall he was. Tall and goofy. I'd seen him stumble and trip and bump into things more times than I could count.

"We're going to try to run a few plays," Kia said.

"Do you want me to go high post or low post?" Ned asked.

"What?" Kia asked, reflecting my own shock at what he'd said.

"Do you want me to go high post or low post? Am I using those words wrong?" Ned asked.

"No, not at all. I just didn't know you knew about stuff like that," she said.

"I didn't until I reached chapter seven in the book. It stated that the center, also known as the big man, or the number five, should always set up in the post.

I just assumed I'd be the center because I'm so much bigger than everybody else."

"Sure, you're the center."

"So do you want me to set up high post or low post?"

"I think low post would be better. Just go over to—"

"About here," Ned said, taking up at just about the correct spot to the right of the hoop. "There were diagrams in the chapter," he explained.

"Good. Now what's going to happen is that I'm going to set up a play. I'm going to send the ball out to Mark. He'll send it back to me and then I'm going to send a chest pass in to you. Understand?"

He nodded his big head.

"And then you have two choices. You can either put the ball up for the net, try to score, or you can pass it back out to one of us."

"Depending on whether the other team doubles down on me and who they leave open," Ned said.

"Yeah, that's right," Kia said.

"Chapter five described the double team and how to break it up by searching for the open man," Ned explained.

"Did you read that book or memorize it?" I asked as I got up from the ground.

"Usually I do both. I have a photographic memory. I remember everything I read or see or hear."

"Everything?"

"Pretty well."

"Ned, it looks like you're going to be quite the player," Kia said.

She was saying those words to Ned, but she was actually looking at and talking to me.

"Okay, shall we try it?" Kia asked.

Mark broke around Ned, using him as a screen, and went to the top of the key. Kia shot him in the ball. He faked a shot—making his invisible man jump up into the air—and then passed to Kia. She grabbed the ball, turned and passed to Ned, and the ball hit him squarely in the middle of his face! He toppled over backward, like a tree being chopped down, his glasses flew through the air and blood exploded out of his face!

"Oh my goodness!" Kia screamed.

"Ned, are you okay?" I yelled.

He was sprawled out on the driveway, his hands covering his face, blood just flowing out from between his fingers.

"I'll get some ice!" Kia yelled and started to run for the house.

"Get lots of ice!" I yelled after her. His nose looked even bigger than it had been a few minutes ago.

\*\*\*

"You feeling any better?" I asked.

"A little bit," Ned said. He was still clutching an ice bag to his face.

"I'm so sorry," Kia said. "Especially about your glasses."

They had split in two, right down the middle on the bridge.

"That's okay," Ned said. "They were already broken and I had them held together with Crazy Glue."

"We have some of that," I said. "Maybe we can fix them."

Even better, maybe we could fix them and get the ice bag off his face before our mothers came back from their walk. I hadn't thrown the ball, and it certainly wasn't my fault that he was such a nerd that he couldn't catch a ball, but I knew that somehow this would be my fault.

I looked anxiously at my watch. They'd left just a few minutes before he'd gotten hurt and were supposed to be gone for a walk through the neighborhood and that was about twenty minutes ago...so...

"Here, let me take the ice away," I said as I pulled away the bag. "It's not good to keep cold on it too long," I offered as an excuse.

I took the bag into the kitchen and dumped it in the sink. I pulled over a chair and pushed it over to the fridge so I could get up into the cupboards above it. That was where we kept all the different types of glues in the house. I rummaged around until I found the little vial that contained the super-stick glue—the stuff that can hold back a charging elephant.

My hope was that Ned's glasses would be back on

his face and we'd all be on the driveway bouncing a ball before our mothers got back. Not that I wouldn't tell them about what happened—later on—but it would be a lot better if they were told about it rather than seeing it themselves.

"I'm so sorry about hitting you in the face like that," Kia said for about the tenth time.

"I think he gets the idea," I said. "Besides it wasn't like you were trying to hurt him. Why didn't you put your hands up?"

"I did. But I thought it was going to be a chest pass," he said.

"It was."

"But it hit me in the face. I had my hands at my chest to catch it," he said.

I shook my head. "It's called a chest pass because you *throw* it from your chest."

"Oh, I didn't understand."

"Maybe that part was in the two pages you didn't get to finish before you played."

"Let me see if I can fix your glasses," Kia said, taking the glue from my hands.

"Maybe I should do it," Ned offered. "I've had lots of practice. I'm always bumping into something and knocking my glasses off. I've broken them four times already this summer."

Kia handed him the glue.

"Where's Mark?" I asked.

"He went out to practice shooting," Kia said. "He

mumbled something about how we're really going to need his shots to drop."

"No doubt there." I turned to Ned. "Are you going to come back outside to play?"

"I don't know. Maybe I should stay in here and read some more about basketball."

"I think playing would be better," Kia said encouragingly. "You can't let one ball in the face hold you back. Right, Nick?"

"Yeah, sure, whatever."

"Remember two seasons ago during the playoffs when Julius Johnson played when he was so sick with the flu that he could hardly walk?"

"Who's Julius Johnson?" Ned asked.

Kia and I looked each other in total shock.

"Is he some sort of basketball player?" Ned asked.

"Some sort of basketball player?" I echoed back. "No, he's not *some sort* of player. He's the best player in the game."

"One of the best players in the *history* of the game," Kia added.

"Oh," Ned said. "I guess maybe I have heard of him."

"How could you not have heard of him? He's amazing. He's on the highlight reel on *Sports Desk* every night."

"*Sports Desk?*"

"It's a TV show. Haven't you ever seen it?"

He shook his head.

"What sort of shows do you watch?" I asked. He probably only watched the Learning Channel.

"I don't," he said, shaking his head. "We don't have a TV."

"You don't have a TV?" I asked in amazement. I didn't think anything in the whole world could be more shocking than him not knowing who Julius Johnson was. I was obviously wrong.

"Why don't you have a television?" Kia asked.

"We're too far out to get any signals."

"What about satellite TV?" Kia questioned.

He shook his head. "That doesn't work either because of how close we are to the mountains."

While all of this was unbelievably strange, it at least helped explain Ned. Who he was and why he was that way now made more sense to me.

"Ned, have you ever seen a basketball game? Either in real life or on TV?" I asked.

"Maybe once…a long time ago. I think it would be an interesting game to watch. I bet there's lots of action."

I didn't know what to say. Kia and I just looked at each other. If he'd just said he was an alien life form visiting from another planet, we couldn't have been any more shocked or surprised than we already were.

"Ned, you should come back outside. Even if you're nervous about playing, you should at least watch us play," Kia said.

"I guess that would be okay."

"And if I do throw you another pass," she said, "it's okay to move your hands to try and catch it."

"Do you think you can memorize that?" I asked.

"I'll try…I'll really try."

# Chapter Seven

"I brought out something for you boys…and girl, to drink," Debbie said as she came out carrying a tray with a pitcher and glasses on it.

"Thanks," Kia said, tossing me the ball.

"Could we show my mom a play before we stop?" Ned asked.

"Sure, why not," Kia said. "I'll sit out while you three run the play."

I knew Kia's offer wasn't so much about being nice as about being the first one to the drinks. We'd been working all day. Ned had made some progress. For one thing, he managed to go the entire day without once catching the ball with his face. Actually, in the beginning he found it difficult to catch the ball with any part of his body, including his hands, but he had improved a little. He'd learned most of the plays, or at least could tell us what they were and what he was supposed to do. He had a lot of trouble doing anything once he got there, but he had thrown the ball up a couple of times and made a basket. The first time I thought it was just an accident or fluke. When he missed the next six—failing to even hit the backboard—I knew I was right. But at least he was trying.

Actually I found Ned very trying. He was trying my patience and trying my ability to remain even remotely polite. It wasn't just that he couldn't play—and he couldn't—as much as the things that kept on coming out of his mouth. He kept rambling on and on about insects, and dinosaurs, and "interesting" facts about nature that nobody but him seemed to find interesting.

I had to hand that to him though. Despite the fact that he stunk, he just kept on trying. He was terrible, but he wasn't giving up. If I was that bad I would have gone inside the house and just quit. Maybe he wasn't smart enough to realize just how bad he was.

There was no question about how much playing time he was going to get in the tournament. Unless the other team totally sucked or we were up by ten baskets, he was going to sit on the sidelines.

Kia had been bugging me, saying we could play him a little. I figured the "littler," the better.

"Can we do one where I get to shoot?" Ned asked.

"Okay. Sure," I answered. What difference did it make?

55

Ned gave me a big goofy smile—which went along perfectly with his big goofy everything. His hair was sticking up into the air in a million directions, and he had this T-shirt that read "Science is happening here!" and wore hiking shorts and canvas hiking shoes. He couldn't have looked goofier if he sat down and planned it out.

"Let's do loosy-goosy," I said.

Mark started with the ball. "Loosy-goosy," Mark called out in his quiet way.

We'd been asking him to yell out the plays, but yelling just wasn't part of Mark. My father said that Mark was so polite and quiet that if you hit him in the face with a shovel, he wouldn't yell "ouch."

"What play was that?" I asked.

Mark shot me a little smile. He knew what I meant.

"Loosy-goosy!" he called out a little louder.

I broke to the ball and Mark bounced a pass to me. He cut toward the hoop and brushed past Ned, who was in the high post, heading for low post. I took the ball and lobbed it up in the air to Ned. I had visions of the ball hitting him in the face in front of his mother so I tossed it as lightly as possible. Ned caught the ball, turned and threw it up at the basket. It clunked off the backboard.

"Rebound!" I yelled out.

Ned jumped up in the air, grabbed the ball and—

"AAAAAHHHHH!" Mark screamed as Ned came

down on top of him, tumbling over backward as he landed.

"Mark, are you okay?" I yelled.

"Of course, I'm not okay!" he screamed.

I'd never heard Mark yell like that before—heck, I'd never even heard him raise his voice. He was definitely not okay. He rolled around on the ground, holding onto his left ankle.

"Let me look at him," Debbie said. "I'm trained in first aid."

She kneeled down beside Mark. Gently she removed his shoe. As she started to take off his sock, he grimaced in pain.

I wanted to look away, like I was afraid that when she removed his sock there'd be a bone sticking out or something. Instead I kept looking. There wasn't a bone, but it looked like he'd swallowed a balloon and it had sunk down to his foot. It was swollen and getting bigger before my eyes. She continued to examine Mark's foot, feeling it with her hands, moving it around and asking Mark questions.

"I don't think it's broken, but it's definitely sprained," Debbie said as she held his foot in her hands.

"It hurts like crazy!" Mark exclaimed. "Like crazy!"

"You'll have to go to the hospital to be checked out, but I'm certain it's only a sprain," she said. "I've had training, not to mention all the practice I've had treating Ned for his falls, bumps and sprains and strains."

Ned was now standing by the pole holding up the backboard. He was craning his neck to see around his mother without getting too close. In his hands were his glasses. They were in two pieces again. When he'd landed on Mark, they'd flown off and hit the pavement. He looked both worried and confused.

"Let me help you up," Debbie said.

Mark got up hesitantly. He tried to put a little weight on his injured ankle, but couldn't.

"We need some ice," Debbie said. "Can somebody come and hold Mark's foot and keep it elevated."

"I will," Kia said. She moved over and took Debbie's place.

"Maybe somebody else too. Ned come and hold him on the other side," Debbie suggested.

"I'll do it," I said, coming over before Ned could even move.

Debbie rushed into the house to get the ice.

I looked right at Ned. "As far as I'm concerned, you've already done enough for today."

***

The phone rang.

"I'll get it!" I said, jumping up from the table.

"Just let it ring and the machine will get it," my mother said. "We've all just sat down for dinner."

"It might be Mark," I said. "I want to know how he is."

"Go and get it," my mother said.

I rushed out of the room, into the living room and grabbed the phone just as it started to ring for the fourth time.

"Hello!"

"Hi, Nick, it's me," Mark said.

"How are you? Is it broken?"

"Not broken. Sprained, just like Ned's mother said it was."

I felt relieved…except a little part of me wanted it to be broken. Not only because I wanted Debbie to be wrong, but I wanted Ned to have done something really bad.

"I guess that's good," I said. "What does that mean …can you play?"

"I have to be on crutches for the next two days and won't be able to put much weight on it for a week or so."

"Then you're out of the tournament…we're all out of the tournament."

"Sorry."

"It's not your fault. It's all Ned's."

"It was an accident," Mark said softly.

"Maybe it was, but if the big freak didn't have feet the size of boats, he wouldn't have tripped over them and landed on you."

"I might be able to walk by Saturday," Mark said.

"But not run or cut or set up for a shot."

There was a long pause. "I'll come down and watch you play."

"Watch us play? Watch who play?"

"You and Kia and Ned."

"You don't really think that we're still going to play, do you?"

"I don't know…I thought maybe."

"We'd just be a joke. I've got to go now. We're having supper."

"Okay. Tell Ned I'm okay. He looked worried. And tell him I know it wasn't his fault."

"Talk to you later," I said and put down the phone.

I walked back into the kitchen. Everybody stopped talking.

"Was it Mark?" my father asked.

"Yep."

"And how is he?"

"In a lot of pain," I said. I didn't care what Mark said. I wanted Ned to feel bad. He should feel bad after what he did to Mark and the team.

"Is it broken?" Debbie asked.

"No. Sprained. A bad sprain…*really* bad."

"Poor Mark."

"Maybe we should go over and see him," Debbie suggested.

"I don't think he wants any visitors right now," I said. "He's still in too much pain."

"I know Ned feels terrible about everything," Debbie said.

I looked over at Ned. He did look like his dog had died. Good.

"Mark knows that it was an accident. He's such a nice boy he wouldn't even be angry about it," my mother said. "Right, Nick?"

"How would I know," I lied. "I'm not psychic."

"But you know Mark."

"But I don't know how he feels about being in so much pain and having to miss the tournament."

"That's right, I guess he can't play. I was so worried about him being injured that I didn't even think about that," my mother said. "I imagine he'll be sad about missing it."

"No sadder than the rest of us are about missing it," I said.

"Missing it?" my father questioned. "Aren't you still going to enter? As long as you have a note from his doctor explaining why he's not able to play, they'll still let you enter the contest with three players."

"What's the point? We don't have a chance without Mark."

"Could you get another player?" Debbie asked.

"Too late. Your team has to be the people listed on the entry form."

"But you three can still play," my mother interjected. "Isn't it about playing? Aren't you and your father always going on about how it's about competing, not about winning?"

"We can't compete. We'd just be a joke…all of us."

"Does Kia feel the same way?" my father asked.

"I haven't talked to her."

"Maybe you should. We've already sent in the forms and paid the entry fee."

"I'd like to still play," Ned said quietly.

"And I'd like it if you *could* play," I snapped.

"Nicholas!" my mother said sternly.

"Could I be excused," I said. "I'm not hungry."

"I think you should be excused. Please go to your room," my mother said.

As I walked out of the room I heard my mother apologizing for me. It wasn't me who needed to be apologized for.

# Chapter Eight

I woke up. What was that sound? I looked over at the other bed. Ned wasn't there. Maybe he couldn't sleep. Served him right. Then I heard it again. What was it? It sounded like a basketball being bounced. I went to the window. It was slightly open, a cool breeze blowing in. The "pinging" of a basketball floated in on the wind. Somebody was bouncing a ball. I looked around as best I could but couldn't see anybody. My room was right over the garage, which stuck out and blocked my view. I glanced at the clock. It was almost two in the morning. Who would be bouncing a ball in the middle of the night? That was just so strange... strange...was it Ned?

Quietly I slipped out of my room. Passing my parents' bedroom I could hear my father. He called it "breathing loudly." My mother called it snoring. There was a little night light on in the upstairs bathroom. The door was open and gave off enough light for me to clearly see my way along the hall and down the stairs. I moved to the front door. It was open. Ned's shoes were no place to be seen in the entranceway, and it was hard to miss things that were that big. He must be wearing them and that meant he must be out there.

I slipped on my shoes. I opened up the door and went outside. The air felt cool and moist and good. I padded down the front path and came around the side of the garage. The ball "pinged" against the asphalt just as I rounded the corner and saw Ned. His back was to me. He was holding the ball high over his head and put up an awkward shot that clanked off the backboard and bounced away. He scrambled after it, catching the ball before it rolled onto the road.

He turned back around and saw me looking at him. He stopped. He looked surprised. Actually he looked surprised most of the time.

"I couldn't sleep," he said.

"I was doing fine until I was woken up by the sound of somebody bouncing a basketball."

"I'm sorry...I didn't mean to wake anybody up."

"Everybody else is still asleep. At least in our house."

"What do you...oh, you mean neighbors," he said, nodding his head.

"You're lucky somebody hasn't phoned the police on you."

"Would they do that?" he asked.

"They could. There are laws against disturbing the peace in the middle of the night."

"I just didn't think about it. I'm not used to having neighbors."

"You're not used to a lot of things," I said pointedly.

Ned didn't answer, but even in the dim light thrown by the streetlight I could tell my jab had hit.

"I just wanted to play a little," Ned said. "I really like the sound the ball makes when it hits the pavement."

"Me too, I've always…" I stopped myself. The sound of the ball bouncing and sneakers squeaking were two of my favorite sounds in the world. "It's okay."

"I just thought I'd come out and practice a little. I guess nobody would argue about me needing to practice."

"Nobody sane."

"It's just nice to be out here without all the people around," Ned said.

"All what people?"

"All everybody. Don't you find it bothers you that everywhere you look there are people and noises? How do you think with everything going on around you?"

"This isn't busy. This is the suburbs."

"It's just nice to have silence sometimes," Ned said.

"It would be quieter if you didn't…" I let the sentence trail off.

"Talk so much?" he asked.

My mother wasn't around. "Yeah, talk so much."

"My mother says I do that when I'm nervous."

"What are you nervous about?" I asked.

"Everything. At least everything here. Could I ask you a question?" Ned asked.

I shrugged in response.

"Why don't you like me?"

"It's not that I don't…," I started to say, but didn't finish. "Lots of reasons."

"Could you tell me…please," he asked.

"Well, for starters, you hurt my friend Mark."

"That was an accident, but you didn't like me before that, did you?"

"Not really."

"I guess I can be annoying sometimes."

"Sometimes?" I questioned.

"Maybe more than sometimes. It's just that I'm not used to having kids around to talk to, so when I do, I don't know what to talk about."

"Try anything except bugs. Nobody likes bugs."

"I like bugs."

"Nobody but you. No bug talk, okay?"

He nodded his head.

"And less talk about everything. Just be quiet sometimes."

Again he nodded his head. "You're so lucky living here. You have friends."

"I'd have more if you'd stop landing on them."

"I really didn't mean to hurt him, honestly!"

"I know," I said. "And so does Mark. He's not even mad at you or nothing…he told me to tell you that. Can I ask *you* a question?"

He shrugged. "Sure, I guess."

"I know you probably like living where you do, out in the forest—"

"It's very pretty," he said.

"I'm sure it is. But living there with nobody around and no TV and not even school. Don't you feel lonely sometimes?"

Ned shook his head. "Not sometimes…I feel lonely all the time. All the time."

I suddenly felt like somebody had kicked me in the stomach.

"Pass me the ball," I said.

Ned bounced the ball to me. "A bounce pass," he said.

"I know," I said.

"Oh, yeah, right, of course. I just was reading and—"

"Here," I said, firing a pass back to him. "Do you know when to use a bounce pass?" I asked.

"When you don't want to use a chest pass?"

I chuckled. "When you're playing against a bigger guy. I'd use a bounce pass to get a ball by you, but if you were on my team I'd always use a chest pass to get the ball high to you like this."

I fired the ball and to my surprise he caught it.

"Turn around and shoot it," I said.

He spun on one foot and threw up the ball. It hit the backboard, missing the rim completely.

"That wasn't too bad," I said, and Ned smiled.

I went after the rebound and brought it back, the ball "pinging" off the pavement as I bounced it.

"I want you to try something else. I'm going to fire the ball to you. I want you to pretend to shoot, but instead fire it back out to me."

"Chest pass or bounce pass?" he asked.

"You decide."

I lobbed in a high pass to Ned. He spun around and made an awkward-looking fake shot and then threw the ball out to me. I put up a long three-point shot, which sailed into the net.

"Nice shot!" Ned said. "I wish I could do that."

"I wish I could do it more often. You've got to remember that I've been playing for a lot longer than three days."

"I'll remember. Do you think we can go over and see Mark tomorrow?"

"Maybe. It depends on how much work we get done tomorrow."

"Work? What sort of work?"

"Unless you think you've already mastered all you need to know for the tournament."

"The tournament? You mean we're going to still enter the contest?"

"We might as well. We've already paid the entry fee so we might as well go…if that's okay with you."

"I'd like that a lot. I just hope I don't embarrass everybody too much."

"So do I," I said. "But we still have two days to work with you…and I guess three nights. There's one more play I want to show you tonight before we go back to bed."

# Chapter Nine

"So let me get this straight," Kia said. "Suddenly you think that we can make Ned into a basketball player."

"I'm not saying a *good* basketball player. I'm just saying a basketball player."

"He's pathetic."

"Keep it down," I said. "You don't want him to hear. You might hurt his feelings."

"Since when are you worried about hurting Ned's feelings?" Kia asked.

"Since...well...you make it sound like I'm a mean person."

"You're not," she said. "To anybody except Ned."

"Well, now I'm going to be nice to everybody, including Ned."

"Does this have anything to do with the fact that we need him or we can't be in the tournament?"

"Maybe a little, but it's just…just…I don't know…I feel sort of…he isn't a bad guy, you know."

Kia shrugged. "I never thought he was. I just thought he was a bad basketball player, and that's a problem."

"We still have two days to work with him, and I showed him some things last night."

"You were practicing without me?" she asked.

"It was late and I didn't want to wake you up."

Kia gave me a questioning look.

"Really late. Let me show you." I turned to Ned. "Let's run the special play," I said.

Ned nodded and gave me a goofy smile. He ran out to high post and put his hands high in the air. I threw up a soft high pass. It didn't have to be hard because nobody we'd be playing would be able to reach that high anyway.

He grabbed the ball and threw it right back to me. As soon as he let go of the ball, he slid down the key to the low post position. I tossed another lob pass to him, he turned and clanked it off the backboard, hitting the rim and bouncing away.

"Except for the end, that wasn't bad," Kia said.

"Nobody gets everything in the net," I said, defending Ned. "We call it the Monarch."

"The Monarch?"

"Like the butterfly," Ned explained. "I spread my wings up high, and then I migrated down the key from high to low post."

Kia gave me the strangest look.

"It wasn't my idea, but it works," I said. "Let's just concentrate on a few plays, nothing too fancy."

"And do things with screens," Ned suggested. "I'm really good with screens."

"Since that only involves standing around and being big, you're a natural," Kia joked.

"That's what Nick said too!"

"Okay, we'll build in a bunch of screen plays," I said.

"Thanks," Ned said. "Thanks a lot…both of you. I'll try not to let you down."

\*\*\*

"I don't know about you two but I need a drink," I said.

"Me too," Kia agreed.

"I'm going to stay out and practice," Ned said.

Kia and I sat down in a shady spot just off to the side. There was already a pitcher of lemonade and three glasses waiting for us. As we poured the drinks we watched Ned. He was taking up a spot on the low post on the left side. He threw up a ball. It missed. He went and got it and awkwardly dribbled back to the same position. He put up the ball again. Again it missed.

"He certainly is persistent," Kia said.

"You have no idea," I said.

Kia knew we'd been practicing late last night, but

I hadn't told her how late or for how long. She would have thought we were crazy. She would have thought I was crazy.

Ned had retrieved the ball again. He put it up and it dropped!

Kia started clapping and I joined in. Ned looked over and smiled at us.

"Do you think we have any chance whatsoever in the tournament?" Kia asked.

"Sure. I think we have two chances. Slim and none. But it beats not being able to play at all. It might even be more fun this way," I said.

"What do you mean?"

"Before, when it was you and me and Mark and Jordan, there was pressure. Like we were supposed to do well."

"We would have done great!" Kia said.

"Maybe. Maybe not. But everybody expected us to do well. Now? Nobody expects anything out of us, so we can just have fun. We could watch other games, or participate in some sort of the activities, like two-ball, or other contests."

"I never thought of that," Kia said.

"We can relax and have a good time."

"You're never relaxed about basketball," Kia said.

"I know, but I am about this. Not having a chance makes things easier."

"Still, it would be nice to win a game, or at least not lose badly."

"It could happen," I said.

"Do you think so?"

"Not really, but it could. Depends how bad the other teams are. Besides, miracles do happen."

We sipped from our drinks and watched as Ned continued to work on his shot.

"You wouldn't mind if I tried to figure out how we could win, would you?" Kia asked.

"Be my guest."

I took another big sip from my drink.

"You know what we could fix?" Kia asked.

"Lots of things."

"We could make Ned look more like a basketball player," she said.

"I thought we were trying to do that."

"No, no, we're trying to teach him to act like a basketball player. I think he should *look* more like one. I think he needs a fashion make-over."

"What did you have in mind?" I asked.

"Look at him. The shorts, shirt, shoes, hair, glasses."

I looked at Ned. Of course she was right. He looked less like a basketball player than anybody I'd ever seen on a court.

"Could you lend him one of your basketball shirts?" Kia said.

"I could, but it wouldn't fit him," I said. "But my father has a couple of jerseys."

"That would be great. And what size shoes does your father wear?"

"Eleven."

"Do you know what size Ned takes?"

"About the same, I think."

"Can he borrow a pair of your father's shoes?"

"Why not? He wouldn't mind."

"And he needs a headband, something to stop his hair from sticking in every direction, and I was thinking we could do something about those shorts and—"

"The socks," I said, cutting her off. "We definitely have to do something about those socks."

"Exactly," Kia said. "Hey, Ned! Come here, we have a couple of ideas."

He trotted over enthusiastically.

***

"Well?" Kia asked.

I shrugged my shoulders. "I guess we'll soon find out."

"Hurry up, Ned!" Kia called through the closed washroom door.

Almost instantly the door opened.

"Wow!" Kia exclaimed.

"Do I look alright?" Ned asked.

"You look like a ball player," I said.

His T-shirt had been replaced by one of my father's jerseys. It fit pretty good. On his head, holding his hair back was a headband. Kia had taken a pair of scissors to his shorts and "modified" them so they looked

quite funky. He had on a pair of white basketball socks and on his feet were a pair of my father's high-topped basketball shoes.

"How are the shoes?" I asked.

"A little bit too big, but they feel pretty light, and sort of bouncy," he said, moving up on his tiptoes and rocking up and down.

"They're designed to be that way. Let's go outside and check them out."

Ned practically ran down the hall and out the door. We trailed after him. He was already on the driveway and he was bouncing up and down.

"These are amazing!" he yelled as he continued to jump around.

I couldn't help but laugh. It was funny watching him, sort of like watching a puppy dog prancing around and chasing after a butterfly—maybe a monarch butterfly.

"So what do you think, Kia?"

She put a hand under her chin and studied him from top to bottom, nodding her head.

"He does look like a player...except for the glasses."

She had a point. They didn't fit the image.

"Ned!" Kia called out. "Do you need those glasses?"

"I can't read without them."

"But can you see without them?" she asked.

"Some things, but I can't see up close without them."

"Take them off," she said.

He pulled them off his face.

"Can you see the net?" she asked.

He looked over, turned back and nodded his head.

"Clearly?"

"Pretty clear."

"How about us?" Kia asked.

"A little blurry, but pretty good."

Kia bent down and picked up the ball.

"Catch!" she yelled.

Ned was still holding his glasses with one hand, but managed to grab the ball with the other. That impressed me.

"Obviously you saw the ball coming, okay."

He nodded.

"In that case I want you to lose the glasses."

"Lose them? My mother will kill me if I lose another pair of glasses!"

"No, no, you don't understand," she said. "I don't want you to *lose* them, I want you to *lose* them."

"She means she wants you not to wear your glasses while you're on the court," I explained.

"Okay," he said.

Kia took the glasses from him and put them down on the table.

"*Now* he looks like a ball player," she said, and she was right.

# Chapter Ten

"Nick, are you awake?" Ned asked.

I turned over in bed. "I was just drifting off."

"I'm too nervous to sleep. Are you nervous?"

"Nope," I said, and I wasn't, which was surprising.

"I guess you get used to it when you play all the time," Ned said.

"I guess," I said. Actually I was always nervous before a game and *had* been really worried about this contest. Now there was nothing to be nervous about. We had no chance. We were just going down to have some fun.

"I was just thinking. What if we get to the finals and I screw up?" Ned asked.

I wanted to say something about us having no chance of getting that far but didn't—what was the point of taking that away from him.

"You won't screw up," I finally said.

"Thanks…but I could."

"We won't let you screw up," I said.

"Thanks."

"We've worked hard the past few days. You've worked hard."

"Thanks. And I have gotten better…right?"

"A lot better. You're a lot better than I was after only playing for four days."

"Really?" he asked.

"Really. Of course I was only about five years old, but you've learned quickly."

I rolled over and looked at Ned. He was lying on the little cot, his feet hanging over the edge, his arms folded under his head. Right beside the bed were his new shoes. His mother had gone out and bought them for him. They were his first pair of basketball shoes. It had been almost funny going with them to the store and helping to pick them out. It wasn't just Ned who didn't know anything about basketball.

"My mom says she is going to get my dad to build me a net when we get home," Ned said.

"That's great."

"I can practice my shooting."

He really needed to practice his shooting. He could make an occasional shot—which was a lot better than he could do three days ago—but it was still only an occasional shot. His shooting was so poor that we'd built almost all our plays around the idea that he wouldn't be putting up any shots.

"My mother said she'd even let me dribble the ball in the house in the kitchen."

"Whatever you do, don't try that here," I warned him. "My mother would kill you."

"I'll try to remember." He paused. "I have my new shoes, and I'll have a hoop, and I've got a ball. All I'll need is somebody to play basketball with."

"That would be good."

"How about you?"

"How about me what? I've got lots of people to play with."

"I meant, would you like to come out and spend some time at my place?"

"You live on the other side of the country, it's not like I can ride my bike over before dinner," I said.

"I know. My mother said it would be okay with her if you came back with us and spent some time."

"In the forest?"

"In our house in the forest. It's really different than here, but beautiful."

"I'm sure it is."

"There's a stream not far from the house where we can go swimming and fishing, and we can go hiking, and there's a patch were we can pick fresh berries... and you don't have to worry because I know how to keep an eye open for the bears and—"

"You have bears?"

"Mostly black bears, but we have grizzlies around sometimes too."

"I read something about how you should always wear a little bell when you're hiking in bear country because it scares them away. Is that true?" I asked.

"Yep. The bears hear the bell and go away. They're more afraid of you than you are of them," Ned said.

"Do you wear a bell?"

"No."

"Why not?" I asked.

"It scares away the bears, but it attracts the mountain lions because they want to see what's making the noise."

"Mountain lions! You have mountain lions?"

"Not a lot, but some. But you don't have to worry, I can take care of you...the way you've taken care of me."

"You know, Ned, I don't even know if my mother and father would let me go."

"But if they did?" Ned asked.

"I guess that maybe I'd think about it," I said. While part of me really didn't want to go, and another part was actually afraid to go, a big part of me thought that maybe it might be fun. Ned wasn't such a bad guy.

"I think what we better do is go to sleep," I said. "Tomorrow is a big day and we have to be ready."

"I'm ready. At least as ready as I can be, I guess."

"Good, then let's go to sleep."

I turned back toward the wall and tried to snuggle down into my sheets. I thought about what it would be like to be away from my family for a while, staying with Ned and his family, living out in the middle of the forest. It certainly wasn't the life I wanted to live. But maybe it would be fun for a week.

"Nick?" Ned called out.

I rolled over.

"Do you want to go out and shoot some baskets?"

I looked at the clock. It was almost midnight and judging from the quiet in the house everybody else was already asleep.

"Do you?" he asked. "It would help me sleep."

I sat up. "Just for a little while."

# Chapter Eleven

"I can't get over all the traffic," Debbie commented.

"This is nothing," my father said.

He and Ned's mother were driving me, Kia, Mark and Ned to the tournament. My mother hadn't come down—she said it made her too nervous to watch. She did, however, want us to call her after every game and tell her the score.

"There are just so many cars everywhere," Debbie said. "I just can't get over it."

"If you want to see traffic, you should try to drive downtown during rush hour on a weekday instead of on a Saturday morning," my father continued.

"I just can't imagine what that would be like," she said.

"Scary," Ned said. "It would be scary."

"Ned, you don't have your glasses," his mother said from the front seat.

"I lost 'em."

"You lost another pair!" she exclaimed.

"No, no, he didn't lose them," I said. "He means he's not using them. Right, Ned?"

"No, actually I did lose them. I couldn't find them when I got up this morning."

"You had them last night," I said. Ned had worn them when we went down to shoot hoops. "I think you left them on that little plastic table on our porch."

"Are you all feeling good this morning?" my father asked.

"Great!" Kia said.

"Pretty good," Ned added.

"Okay," Mark said.

He wasn't going to be able to play, but he was coming to cheer us on. Mark was like that. He didn't need the crutches any more but he was still limping.

"And you, Nick?

"I just wish we had a little more time to practice our plays."

"It seems like there never is enough time. Did you do the best that you could?" my father asked.

"We did," I said, and we had.

Nobody could have practiced more than we had over the past few days. That was the problem. We'd been preparing for days. Other people had spent weeks or months. And of course all our practice had been on our own. We didn't have anybody to play against, so we only hoped that what we'd planned would work.

"I think we're going to win," Ned said.

"That's the attitude!" Debbie chirped. "Think positive!"

I was *positive* that we weren't going to win. Maybe Ned needed to be prepared for that...or maybe I could just keep my mouth shut and let him believe for a little bit longer.

"A positive attitude is good," my father said, "but that has to be combined with a realistic attitude."

Thank you, I thought, but didn't say anything.

"The best teams from across the whole city are going to be here today," my father continued.

"We're not worried," Kia said.

"I don't want you to worry. I just don't want you to be disappointed," my father added.

I didn't think that would be a problem. When you don't expect to win any games, there isn't much that can disappoint you.

Our van slowed down and joined a line of cars waiting to go into the exhibition grounds.

"This is something I can't get used to," Debbie said. "Waiting in line and being crowded in."

"This isn't too bad," my father said.

"Not bad for here maybe. Up where we come from if you pass more than two cars every hour it's rush hour."

My father paid nine dollars to a parking attendant and eased the car into a spot in the lot. It was still only eight thirty, a full hour before our first game, but already the lot was half filled.

"What do we do now?" I asked.

"We go and register," my father said.

"I thought we'd already done that."

"We sent in the registration forms. Now we have to let them know your team is here and they check your identification."

"To see that we're the right age...right?"

"Exactly."

My father turned to Debbie. "You did bring his birth certificate, right?"

"I have it right here," she said. "I'm used to having to show it to people. Nobody ever believes he isn't older."

We crossed over a street, moving between other cars and trucks waiting to park. Up ahead I could see the courts—lots and lots of courts. Stretching out ahead set up in a parking lot were dozens and dozens of hoops.

We passed by the first court. It had a little sign—Court 22—above it. The backboard was covered with an ad for a shoe company. I looked at the next backboard, and the next, and the next. Each one was covered by an advertisement. It seemed like if you could wear it, bounce it, drink it, or play it, it was advertised on one of the backboards. Maybe they should—

"Ouch!" I said as Ned bumped into me.

"Sorry," he apologized. "I was just looking around... there's so many people...so much to see. How many courts are there?"

"I don't know, but I see a sign above that far one and it says sixty-six, so at least that many," I said.

"They have to have that many. I heard there are going to be over six hundred teams here today," Kia said.

"We're competing against six hundred teams!" Ned exclaimed.

"No, of course not. That's how many teams there are in all categories, all ages and both boys' and girls' teams."

"There are girls' teams?" Ned asked. "But…" he motioned to Kia.

"We're a boys' team. Think of me as a boy…just smarter and better-looking."

"Girls can be on a boys' team. Boys can't be on a girls' team," I explained.

"Do you know how many teams will be in our category?" Ned asked.

"We'll find out when we get our schedule," my father said. "Here's the registration booth."

We stopped in front of an open-sided tent. There were tables at the sides and gigantic charts on the walls. Each chart represented one category. That was where all the scores would be listed after each game.

I turned around to watch the activities while my father registered us. It had only been a few minutes since we started our walk across the area, but already it had gotten busier. A few kids were taking shots at different hoops. A big refreshment stand—the sign said it sold dogs, burgers and cold drinks—opened up. A machine was turned on with a loud hiss and a gigantic inflatable basketball, already the size of a small house, was rising up.

"I can't believe how busy it is," Ned said. "There must be a couple of hundred people here."

"That's nothing. By the time the first games start, I bet there'll be more than a thousand people here," I said.

"You're wrong," Kia said. "There won't be a thousand people. There'll be thousands and thousands of people."

"That's a lot of people," Ned said.

"That's not that many," I said.

"Maybe not to you, but you have to remember where I come from, the biggest place has only three hundred people who live there, and I have to drive three hours to even find that many people."

"There we are, all registered," my father said, returning with some papers in his hands.

"How many teams in our category?" I asked.

"Twenty-four."

"Twenty-four!" Ned exclaimed.

"Don't worry," Kia said. "Most of them won't be that good."

"I hope not," I said.

"The teams are divided into four divisions, so you've only got five other teams and you play round-robin."

"What does that mean?" Ned asked.

"We play each team once," I said.

"That means we have five games," Ned said.

"And what happens after the round-robin?" I asked.

"As far as I can tell, the top two teams from each division then make the playoffs," my father said.

"So twenty-four teams become eight," Kia said.

"And if we make the playoffs?" Ned asked.

"It looks like the second place team in each division plays one of the teams that finished first in another division. Sudden death."

"Which means that the losing team goes home," Kia said. "So there's only four teams left."

"And those teams play again?" Ned asked.

Kia nodded. "And the winners of those games play in the finals."

"So if we keep winning we could play...five, six, seven, eight games," Ned said.

I had to hand it to Ned. He didn't know much about basketball, but he certainly could do math.

"If we keep winning," I agreed, although I figured five was about all we'd be playing. It was unlikely we'd be top two in our division.

"Enough talking about playing, we'd better get you to your court so you can warm up for your first game," my father said. "You're going to be on court seventy-two. Follow me."

We trailed behind my father as he wove his way toward our court. Although no games had officially started yet, there were people on every court, practicing, taking shots, fooling around. It was obvious that there were lots of different ages and sizes and skill levels. I watched some of the older players as we passed by. Some were putting up shots from the three-point line—shots that were dropping. Others were dunking, the backboard and rim screaming in protest. This would have been fun to watch if I wasn't playing.

"Boy, these guys can play, can't they, Ned," I said.

He didn't answer. I looked around. He was walking off to the side, well away from us, staring at the action.

"Ned!" I yelled.

He popped out of his trance and looked at me. He trotted over.

"What's going on over there?" Ned said, pointing to a set of metal bleachers that were on three sides of one court.

"That's center court," Mark explained. He'd been down here last year. "They have all the contests there."

"Contests?" Ned asked.

"Three-point shooting, two-ball contests, dunking contests," Mark said. "We can come and watch between games and—"

His voice was drowned out by a blast of music. We all turned around. Radio station KIZS 99 had opened up its mobile station and music was blaring out of three gigantic speakers.

"That's really loud!" Ned said.

"Ned, do you know what this reminds me of?" Debbie asked.

He shook his head.

"That time when we went into Dawson Creek because the carnival had come to town."

I looked around. There were people milling all around, loud music, activities, refreshment stands and different attractions. It *did* look like a carnival. All that was missing were the clowns. I just hoped that wasn't going to be us.

# Chapter Twelve

"Okay, gentlemen, and lady," the ref said. "Red team won the coin toss so they get first ball."

Ned looked confused.

"We're the blue team," I said softly.

One team was called blue and the other red even though the three of us were in white and the other team had on gray shirts.

I had one eye on the other team for the entire warm-up. They were pretty good. All four could shoot and dribble. Two of them were the same size as Kia and me. The third was a little shorter and the fourth guy a lot shorter.

I'd also been watching them watching Ned. They huddled together and pointed. They really didn't know if he could play, but they did know that he was more than a head taller than anybody else on the court.

"Before we start, I'm going to give you a quick review. First team to sixteen baskets wins. Shots from behind the three-point line count for two baskets. First seven fouls you get the ball. Fouls eight through twelve you get a shot. Every foul after twelve you get a shot and the ball back. If the game hasn't been decided in thirty minutes, the team with the most points wins. Any change in possession of the ball from one team to the other and the ball must be taken out beyond the three-point line. Any questions?"

"Yeah," one of the members of the other team said. "We want to see his identification."

"There's no way he's our age," piped in a second, pointing at Ned. The third nodded in agreement.

Debbie came onto the court. "Here's his birth certificate," she said, handing it to the ref.

"He is awfully tall," the ref said, studying the card.

"Takes after his father," Debbie said.

"Looks good," the ref said, handing back the card. "Let's play ball."

The ref tossed the ball to their player. "Check it before starting."

As agreed I went out on the player with the ball, Kia covered a second player and Ned took the third.

"Check," their man said as he bounced the ball to me.

I bounced it right back out and we were ready to start.

"Break!" he said, and the two players crossed.

"Switch!" Kia yelled.

Kia's player burst free around Ned and was hit with a pass. He glided in and put up an easy shot for the first basket of the game.

"I called switch! Why didn't you switch?"

"I didn't know what you meant."

"It means that we're supposed to switch men and—"

"Come on blue team this isn't the time for a lesson. Take the ball out," the ref said.

"Remember to yell for the ball," I said out of the side of my mouth as I walked past Ned.

I walked the ball to the top of the court and then checked it.

"Here! Here!" Ned yelled, holding an arm high above his head and the outstretched arm of the player trying to cover him. He was a tempting target.

I turned to look for Kia. She sprinted down, circled Ned and came back out to the top of the key. I tried to send her a pass and it deflected off the hand of the man covering me. Another one of their players grabbed the ball, dribbled out to the three-point line and put up a shot. Straight into the net!

\*\*\*

"That's game!" the ref called out as their shot dropped through the mesh.

We'd lost the game, sixteen to twelve. I hadn't really

expected to win, but somehow I hadn't figured that we'd lose. Of course, that made no sense. I stumbled over and we awkwardly shook hands with the other players. Mark came onto the court to do the same. Even though he hadn't played—and wouldn't be playing the entire day—he was still on our team. Boy, I would have loved to have him out there. Two of his long shots would have won it for us.

"You did wonderfully!" Debbie said as she reached up and gave Ned a big hug. "You all did wonderfully!" she continued as she hugged all of us in turn.

"Better luck next game," my father said quietly. "You want a drink?"

"Sure," I said.

We walked away from everybody else toward one of the refreshment stands.

"That wasn't a bad game," he said.

"Not bad, but not good. Four more to go."

"I thought there could be eight games today?"

I chuckled. "Five is all we're going to play."

"It sounds like you've already quit."

"Well…do you blame me?" I asked.

"I think you probably won't be finishing top two in your division."

"So you agree with me," I said.

"I agree it's going to be tough, but I think you have a chance if you'd spread the ball around a little more."

"We were shooting from all over," I said.

"You and Kia were shooting from all over. You hardly used Ned at all."

"We threw some passes in to him."

"Not many."

"As many as we can risk. He doesn't catch so well."

"He didn't put up a single shot," my father noted.

"And if you'd seen him shoot you'd know that's a good thing."

"But it's not just me who doesn't know he can't shoot," my father said.

"What do you mean?"

"Nobody's seen him play. They look at him and they see a big tall guy dressed like a basketball player."

"Yeah?"

"So looking at him, they think he can play. If you give him the ball more—even if he doesn't shoot—he's going to draw coverage. Then he can get the ball back outside to you or Kia. You can't win without him."

"And we can't win with him either."

"He has gotten better."

"Getting better than he *was* wasn't hard," I agreed. "He was the worst player in the world."

"Was. Thanks to you and Kia he's become better."

"We've spent every day practicing," I agreed.

"Not to mention nights."

"Nights?" I asked.

"You think you're the only one who wakes up in the middle of the night?"

"I didn't know you knew."

"Your mother's and my bedroom overlooks the driveway, remember?"

"But why didn't you make us stop if it was bothering you?"

"I didn't say it was bothering me, I said I heard you. I even watched out the window for a while. It looked like you were having fun." He paused. "Ned really has been trying, hasn't he?"

"For sure."

"And you're been good to him...at least you have for the past few days."

"I've been trying," I said, still feeling badly about how I'd treated him before that.

"He's not a bad kid, is he?"

"No," I said shaking my head. "He's different, but he's okay."

"Then maybe he deserves a chance...even if he can't make the shots...even if you're going to lose... he deserves a chance to at least try to help your team win, don't you think?"

I nodded my head.

"And who knows? Maybe you might just win a game."

"There's a chance. Not a big one, but a chance."

# Chapter Thirteen

I took the ball and walked to the top of the court.

"Check," I said as I bounced the ball out to the player who was covering me. He tossed it back.

"Monarch!" I called loudly.

Kia moved off to the side, taking her man with her. Ned set up in the high post. He towered over the player covering him. Actually even I was taller than all the players on the other team. He raised his arms high, making an easy target.

I took the ball and lobbed a light pass to Ned, well over the leaping hands of the other player. Ned fumbled the ball, and it almost dropped free before he recovered and grabbed it with both hands. All three of their players converged around Ned, jumping up and down, desperately trying to stop him from shooting. He took the ball and tossed it back out to me. There was nobody on me at all, and I aimed and put up the shot. It hit the rim and bounced off! Ned reached up and grabbed the rebound. He turned and fired it out to me. I passed over to Kia. There was nobody on her either and she took aim and fired. It was short, but Ned got the rebound again! He awkwardly lobbed the ball out to me. I shot and this time it dropped.

"Nice shot," Ned said.

"I should have got it the first time."

"All that's important is that you did get it," Ned said.

"Thanks. Go out and cover the throw-in man."

"Me?" Ned asked.

"Yeah, you. Wave your arms around a lot."

I knew that either Kia or I should have gone out and left Ned standing under the hoop, but I was just too tired. It seemed to be getting hotter by the minute and while the other teams could bring in an extra man, we couldn't.

Ned walked out. The man bounced him the ball for the check.

"I got it!" Ned yelled. "I got it!"

The ref blew his whistle. "That was a check. You have to give him back the ball."

Ned looked embarrassed. He handed the ball back to their man.

"Don't worry about it," Kia said. "Just cover him."

\*\*\*

"That's time!" the ref yelled. "Final score eleven to nine."

We shook hands with the other team members. Running out of time hadn't been how I'd figured we'd win—heck I hadn't even figured we'd win—but I didn't care. That evened things up at one win and one loss.

"So was that better?" I asked my father.

"Better and smarter. As long as you keep feeding Ned inside, he'll draw people off of you and Kia. It doesn't matter if he can't shoot as long as they don't know he can't and keep covering him."

"I need to sit down," Kia said.

"Me too," I agreed.

We started to weave our way across the site. There were games going on at every hoop, crowds gathered at the sidelines watching, little boom boxes playing a jumble of loud competing sounds. As we walked, it felt like we were being bombarded by sounds, and sights, and even the smells from the refreshment stands.

"This is really something, isn't it?" I said, turning to find myself walking alone.

Anxiously I looked around to see everybody else standing before a display behind me. I scrambled back to join them.

"Do you believe the size of those feet?" Kia asked.

In front of us were the running shoes of a whole bunch of NBA players. The exhibit was called "Step into their Shoes." The shoes were sort of anchored to the floor and there were lineups of people waiting to take a turn to try on the different shoes.

"Do you want to try them on?" Ned asked.

"Maybe later. I need to get off my feet and sit down," I said.

"There's a nice spot right over there by that tree," my father said, pointing it out. "Why don't you four go and sit down, and Ned's mother and I will get you all a drink."

"That would be great," Kia said.

We started off in one direction while they went in the other. There were lots of people sitting in the shade, but we managed to find our own little patch on the grass.

"You made some good plays out there," I said to Ned.

"And a lot of dumb ones too. It's harder here than on your driveway."

"It's not just harder, it's hotter," Kia said. "I'm melting."

It was still only ten thirty and I knew it was going to get hotter over the next few hours, but it was already like an oven. The sky was clear and blue and there wasn't a cloud in the sky to block out the sun, which was baking down on the blacktop of the parking lot.

"I was getting tired," Kia said. "We really need a sub."

"Sorry," Mark said.

"So am I," Ned apologized. "I still feel bad about—"

"No sense in worrying about that now. All we can do is play hard for the next three games."

"Maybe we should save something if we play later," Kia suggested.

"If we save anything, we won't be playing later. Let's just keep trying as hard as we can," I said. "After all we've already won one more game than I thought we would."

"You didn't think we were going to win *any* games?" Ned asked. He sounded shocked.

"Well...I really didn't know," I said, squirming for an answer. "I just thought we'd have some fun."

"It is fun," Ned said. "Although it was a lot more fun winning than it was losing."

"It always is," Kia stated. "It always is."

"We've got to stay focused out there," I said. "Those whistles are driving me crazy."

Every court had a ref, and every ref had a whistle, which he blew at each stoppage of play. There were whistles coming at us from every direction and I had to fight the urge to stop at each one.

"It is distracting," Kia agreed.

"Everything's distracting," Ned added. "There's just so much happening all around us. It's hard."

"All we can do is try to block everything out and concentrate on the basketball," I said.

"That's not easy," Kia said. "This isn't like any basketball game I've ever played."

Ned laughed. "It's not like anything I've ever done in my whole life. This is...amazing."

*\*\**

"Timeout!" I panted.

"One minute timeout!" the ref yelled.

I walked over to the side, still carrying the ball. Kia and Ned and even Mark came over and gathered around me.

"Do you have a play in mind?" Kia asked as she slurped down some water.

I shook my head. "I just needed a drink...and a break...I'm really tired."

"Me too," she admitted. "It feels like my feet are on fire. It's getting worse with every game."

"I know. We've just got to push through this last game."

This was our fifth game. We'd won two and lost two. We were down fifteen to twelve. If we won this game we had a chance at finishing second in our division, depending on what was going on in the other games. First place was way out of sight. The team that had beaten us in our first game had already won four games and, from the little bit I'd seen of the game underway on the court next to us, they were well ahead in their fifth game.

"So what are we going to do?" Kia said.

"We need a sub."

"I know we need a sub but—"

"No, I mean we *are* going to sub. Kia you're out and Mark's in."

"Me?" Mark exclaimed. "But I can't run."

"We don't need you to run. Can you stand and shoot?"

"Yeah."

"That's all we need. I'm going to put it in to Ned. You set up outside the three and he'll put it back to you."

"But even if he scores he can't run enough to defend," Kia said.

"Let's just get the basket first and worry about that later. Let's go."

I walked out to the top of the court. Kia stayed on the sidelines as Ned set up low and Mark went way up high.

"New man!" called out one of their players, noticing the change we'd made.

I checked the ball. The instant I got it I lobbed a high ball to Ned. Just as in every game we'd played their whole team collapsed around him like a swarm of bees. He tossed the ball back out to Mark. He had all the time in the world. He took aim and shot the ball, an easy basket and—it hit the rim and bounced off! Ned grabbed the rebound and in one motion put it back out to Mark. Mark shot. This time it dropped for two!

"Sub!" I yelled. "Mark out, Kia in!"

Mark limped off the court in one direction as Kia ran back on from the other sideline. I went up top and checked the ball. He passed it in to Kia's man who tried to drive past her. She reached out and smacked him hard on the arm.

"Foul!" the ref called out. "That's number seven. Take a shot."

If he made the shot, they'd win, and we'd be out of the contest.

"Mark, you're in again," I called out. "I'm out."

As I went to the sideline, I walked right past the player getting ready to take the shot.

"It all comes down to you. Don't choke," I said. "'Cause when you miss the shot, we're going to win."

I grabbed my water bottle and watched as he bounced the ball on the pavement...and then bounced it again. He put the ball up...air ball! He didn't even hit the backboard!

"Take it outside!" the ref called out.

Kia was going to in-bounds the ball. Ned set up in his usual place while Mark took up a spot just outside the three-point line. This time he was being closely covered.

"Break!" Kia yelled.

Ned lumbered up toward her while Mark limped over to the side. It looked painful even to watch him move. She tossed in a high pass to Ned. His defender jumped high in the air but wasn't even close to getting it. Ned faked a shot and then put it out to Mark. He shot and missed. Ned grabbed the rebound.

"Put it up!" my father yelled.

Ned turned around and put up a shot—nothing but net! The game was tied at fifteen!

"Sub!" I screamed.

"You can't substitute with every possession!" the ref called out. "Keep playing."

I was going to say something, but I knew he wasn't going to change his mind.

"Go to a zone!" I screamed.

Mark and Kia backed in toward the net. Ned looked confused.

"Just stay under the net!" I yelled at him and he nodded his head and retreated underneath the hoop.

The other team took the ball to the top. The ball was bounced into Kia who sent it back out to the player.

The whole game was now down to one shot. By playing a zone we were challenging them to take a shot from the outside—but what choice did we have? Mark couldn't run and Ned wasn't quick enough to cover anybody. If they sunk it, they won. If they missed, we'd have a chance to win it.

"Hands up!" Kia screamed and all three of them put their hands up. Ned was stretching up so far it looked like he could almost touch the rim.

They pushed the ball around, first to one man, then the other, and back to the first. They were all open for a shot but it was like they were all afraid to take it, like

they'd rather somebody else was the hero…or the goat. Finally one of their players set, got the ball and got ready to shoot. Kia rushed out and jumped into the air…he faked the shot and dribbled by her…it was just a little ten-footer now! He put the ball up and Ned reached out and smashed it away! It bounced right to Kia who dribbled a few feet out to the line and then threw it back in to Mark. He put up a little shot and it dropped! We'd won! We'd won!

\*\*\*

Silently we watched as a woman at the score-keeping tent listed our score. Some of the other game scores weren't in yet, so we didn't know if we'd be moving on. There were two other teams that still had a chance to finish with the same record as us.

"What happens if we're tied?" Ned asked.

"They have rules to break ties. The first one is head-to-head competition."

"What does that mean?" he asked.

"We beat team six. Even if they win their fifth game and finish with the same record as us, we'll be in and they'll be out."

"So they can't beat us," Ned said.

"They're not the team we're worried about," Kia said. "We have to find out how team seven did."

"That was the fourth team we played, right?" Ned asked.

"That was them. If they won their last game then we're out."

"It can't be long," Kia said. "Even if nobody reaches sixteen baskets the time must almost be up."

"Unless they started late," I said.

We stood off to the side and watched as people brought game sheets over to the scorekeeper's table. She looked at each score and then walked over and recorded each game on the big board.

"I don't see anybody from team seven," Kia said.

"That's good." The winning team was responsible for bringing the sheets over, so as long as we didn't see any of them that would mean that they'd lost and—I saw the four of them walking up. I couldn't wait any longer. I walked over to meet them.

"How did you guys do in your last game?" I asked.

"We did okay," one of them said.

"Oh, so you won?" I asked, trying to hide my disappointment.

"No, we lost by three points, but we played okay."

I had to fight the urge to yell out.

"So how did your team do?" one of them asked.

"We did okay too...we won."

Somehow against all the odds we'd made it to the playoffs!

# Chapter Fourteen

"Look at them eyeing Ned," Kia said to me under her breath.

"It's almost like we're not even here."

Just like before every game, the other team spent most of their time staring at Ned in wonder. We made sure that he didn't take any shots during the warm-ups. The last thing in the world we wanted them to see was that he couldn't shoot. It was enough that he was gigantic and dressed like a ball player.

"Think they'll ask to see his ID?" Kia asked.

"Wouldn't you?" I asked in turn.

So far before every game, Ned's age had been questioned and his mother pulled out his birth certificate.

"Captains, please!" the ref called out.

"You go, Ned," I said.

"Me? I'm not the captain."

"You are for this game. Go for the coin toss."

Ned went out and joined the ref and the captain of the other team.

"They looked pretty good in the warm-ups," Kia said.

"They did," Mark agreed.

"They must be good. They finished first in their division."

"Do you think we can take them?" Kia asked.

"What do you think?" I asked instead of answering.

"I think I'm really tired."

"Me too." I turned to Mark "You feeling like you can go out there a bit this game?"

"I can shoot…I can run a little."

"If we win the coin toss, you're in to start the—"

"It's their ball," Ned said.

"Darn. Mark you're out. First possession you're back in. I'll get the ball back to you for a long shot."

"How about we worry about their first possession first," Kia said.

"Sounds right," I agreed.

\*\*\*

I took the ball up to the top of the court. I walked slowly. I needed to get some wind back in my lungs. Slowly I lobbed it out to their man to check the ball. He passed it back.

"Eight!" I yelled.

Ned was standing at the high post and slid down toward the net. He raised his arms and I tossed a ball out to him. It bounced off one hand and then the other and there was a scramble for the ball! It bounced up in the air and Kia grabbed it! She turned and passed out to me. I put up the ball and it sailed right into the net!

"That wasn't exactly the way we practiced that," I said as I took up a position inside.

"It doesn't matter as long as it worked," Kia said. "We're giving them a game."

\*\*\*

The ball popped loose and I scrambled after it…reaching… reaching…and bang! I smashed together with two of their players and went shooting through the air, landing on my side, the asphalt biting into my leg.

The ref blew his whistle and my father and Debbie rushed out onto the court.

"That doesn't look good," my father said.

I looked down. The whole side of my left leg was scraped up.

"Referee's timeout…sixty seconds."

My father helped me to my feet and I limped over to the sidelines.

"What's the score?" I asked.

"We're down twelve to eleven."

"Maybe we should put Mark back in," I suggested.

"No good," Mark said. "They know I'm going to shoot."

We'd put Mark in five times and each time the ball went out to him for a shot. The first three times it worked. The next two they were covering him, waiting for it. The last time they even stole the ball.

"You're in, but you're not going to shoot. Ned's going to fake the pass out to you."

"And I'm going to send it to Kia, right?" Ned asked.

"No. You're going to shoot."

"Me?"

"Put it up."

"And if I miss?"

"You'll get the rebound and shoot again."

"And if I miss again?"

"Everybody misses. Take the shot."

I sat down while the three of them walked out onto the court.

"Look for the shooter!" one of their players called, pointing at Mark. A man went and practically stood on top of him.

"Check," Kia said as she passed the ball into their man. He put it right back out.

"Break!" Kia yelled.

Ned moved a few feet down to take up a spot down low, right next to the hoop. Mark tried to move, but his ankle wouldn't let him do anything more than hobble. Ned raised his arms and Kia lobbed in a pass.

He grabbed the ball firmly in both hands. He turned and fired the ball up. It went straight into the net! The game was tied!

"Way to go!" I screamed.

Ned yelled and whooped and jumped up and down!

"Zone defense!" Kia called out.

Kia came to the top of the key and Mark hobbled into position in the middle. Ned was already under the hoop. This left the other team completely open all around the edge of the key—free to shoot, and they knew how to shoot. This wasn't going to work. As soon as they scored, I'd sub back in and—

"Time!" the scorekeeper called out. "That's thirty minutes."

Everybody stopped in their tracks. That didn't seem like thirty minutes.

"Two-minute break," the ref said. "Who had first ball?"

"They did," Kia said.

"Then your team starts with the ball."

We walked off the court and gathered around my father and Ned's mother. I went to sit down, but the pavement was too hot. I squatted down instead.

"What happens now?" Ned asked.

"Sudden death. First team to score wins," Kia explained.

"What play are we running?" Mark asked.

"I don't know…Kia?"

She shook her head. "Set up Mark for a shot?"

"That's no good," Mark said. "They're covering me too close and I can't move to get free."

"I understand. Ned, you throw in the ball."

"Me?"

"Him?" Kia questioned.

"Him. Nobody will expect that."

"Nobody including me," Kia confirmed.

"Who do I throw it to?"

"Whoever's open. Let's go."

"Good luck," Mark offered.

We went out onto the court. The other team was already waiting. The ref handed me the ball—he was expecting me to throw it in too. I put it in Ned's hands.

"Don't worry," I said.

"I'm not worried…I'm terrified."

As Ned walked to the top of the court I could see the other team was surprised. They didn't know what to do. The man who had been covering Ned didn't want to go out after him, but wanted to stay underneath the net.

"Remember to check the ball!" I called out.

Ned nodded his head and then handed the ball to the man who was covering him—the man who had been covering me. He was fast, really fast, and had been giving me troubles the whole game. He handed the ball back to Ned.

"Break!" Ned yelled.

Kia and I scrambled, crossing at the top of the key. My man, who was a lot taller than me, wasn't nearly as fast and I left him behind.

"Ned! Ned!" I yelled.

He threw the ball over top of his man. It flew up and over my head, just deflecting off my outstretched fingers. I spun around in time to see Kia grab the ball. She turned, fired and it dropped!

# Chapter Fifteen

The other team didn't just look confident. They looked down right cocky. They warmed up a little, but mainly strutted around the court, looking at us, pointing and laughing. I'd played against people like this before—players who thought basketball was about attitude instead of actually playing. Unfortunately this team had more than just attitude. They'd won all five of the games in the opening round, and then blown away the opposition in the first round of the playoffs. When I saw the score—16 to 3—I thought it had been written down wrong. It wasn't. They'd killed the other team. Maybe they had a right to be confident.

One of them walked up to Ned and stuck a finger in his face. "You're going down!"

"Going down where?" Ned asked.

The kid looked confused. "Down...um, down... like you're going to lose!"

"Maybe," Ned said. "We might. We've already lost two games."

"We're going to do you!"

"Do me what?"

"Beat you. What's with you?"

"Nothing much. What's with you?" Ned asked.

"Are you mouthing off to me?" he demanded.

"I am using my mouth...I don't know how else to talk," Ned said.

"In your face!" the kid yelled.

"What's in my face?" Ned asked.

"Me! I'm going to be in your face the whole game."

"The only way you're going to be in his face is if you brought along a ladder," Kia said, stepping in between the two of them.

"You're soon gonna wish you were smart enough to play on a girls' team," the kid snapped.

"Back off!" the ref barked stepping in between the kid and Kia. "I'm not putting up with any of that stuff you four did in the opening rounds!" the ref said, waving a finger at the other team.

What sort of stuff had they done? The bad feeling I'd had in my gut got worse.

"We're here to play ball, nothing more. Now call the coin toss for the first ball," the ref said.

"We don't want the ball," another one of their

players said. "Let them have it. They need all the help they can get!"

"Gee, thanks," Ned said, reaching out to shake hands with the guy.

He slapped away Ned's hand.

"Technical foul!" the ref bellowed.

"What?"

"Technical foul. They get a free shot and the ball back."

"You can't do that!" yelled a man who stepped out of the crowd.

"I'm the ref, I can do what I want."

"That's my son, and I'm their coach!"

"Now having met you, I can see where he gets his fine manners from. I'm the ref and you better get off my court now or I'll be adding a second technical foul. Do you know what that means?"

"No, what does it mean?" the man demanded.

"Forfeit of the game."

"You can't do that!"

"Yes I *can*. Walk away while you *can*," the ref said calmly.

"You can't threaten me!" the man yelled.

"I'm not threatening. This is a promise. Get off now or the team is disqualified."

The man hesitated then walked off the court, mumbling something I was sure I didn't want to hear.

"Take a shot to start," the ref said, handing me the ball.

"Can anybody take it?" I asked.

"Anybody on the team."

"Sub in," I said, tossing Mark the ball as I walked past him.

He limped over to the line, took aim and sank the shot.

"Sub in," I called out.

I reached out and gave Mark a low five as we passed. Boy, things would have been different if he'd been able to play—not to mention Jordan. There was no telling how far we could have gone. We could have taken these guys.

The ref took the ball and tossed it to me. I walked up to the top of the court.

"Check," I said as I bounced the ball out to my man.

"Check this!" he said as he fired it back in to me, hard. If I hadn't got my hands up in time it would have hit me in the face.

"There's more where that came from, sucker!" he snarled.

I was thrown. What was with this guy?

"Play ball!" the ref yelled. He sounded angry and I wasn't sure if it was with me.

"Buzz!" I called out.

That was a play for Kia to shoot after Ned set a screen to free her up.

Kia broke toward the top of the key as Ned moved down and took up position. Kia slid by Ned and her man crashed into him. I threw the ball to Kia. She turned and threw up a shot before the other man could get to her. The ball went up, well wide of the mark and hit the backboard. The ball dropped almost straight down. Ned leaped up and grabbed the ball and came down, knocking one of their players off to the side and landing heavily on the second as the two of them tumbled over backwards.

"Time!" the ref yelled. He reached down and tried to help one of their players to get up, but he refused his hand and scrambled to his feet.

"That guy nearly killed me!" he screamed. "The big doofus!"

"It was an accident!" I protested.

"You shut up!" a second member of their team yelled at me. He came right up into my face and pushed me and I tumbled over backwards and—

"That's it!" the ref yelled. "Disqualification for the red team!"

I picked myself up as my father and Ned's mother and lots of other people crowded onto the court. It seemed like everybody was yelling and screaming and angry.

"Leave it to the ref," my father said as he grabbed me by the hand. "All of you come over here."

We moved off the court and to the side. We watched from a safe distance as a bunch of adults—that one kid's father and maybe some other parents—continued to yell and scream at the ref. He seemed to be holding his own in the yelling department.

"It was an accident," Ned said. "I fall down a lot."

"I noticed," Mark said quietly.

"I'm so sorry about that and—"

"I'm just joking around, Ned," Mark said.

"We all know you wouldn't try to deliberately hurt somebody," my father said. "You just tripped."

"Why don't they believe that?" Ned asked.

"Because they're jerks!" Kia yelled out.

They were too far away and there was too much yelling going on for them to possibly hear her comment. I was grateful for that.

"Don't worry about them," I said. "There's always some people like that everywhere."

"Really?"

"Of course," I said. "Haven't you ever run into jerks like that before…people looking for a fight?"

"Not really."

"Come on," Kia said. "Not at school…oh, that's right you don't go to school."

"How about in town?" I asked.

He shook his head.

"We don't go to town that often," Debbie said. "And when we do we already know everybody."

"You're friends with everybody in the whole town?" Kia questioned.

"Oh, no," Debbie said. "There are some people I wouldn't even *want* to be friends with, but even people who don't even like each other still wouldn't act like that," she said, pointing at the throng of people surrounding the ref.

A second ref had come over. He was accompanied by two men who were wearing shirts that said "Official." They joined in the discussion. Soon I couldn't hear the words being yelled anymore, although the faces still looked angry. Maybe they were going to come to some sort of agreement and we could start playing again or—the adults stalked off the court, the four boys trailing after them. They were quickly swallowed up by the crowd and disappeared.

"I think that means we're not going to be shaking hands at the end of the game," Kia said.

The ref walked over to us, accompanied by one of the officials.

"Here's the score sheet," he said, handing the sheet to my father. "You win sixteen to zero. The other team is disqualified."

"That's too bad that they had to lose that way," my father said.

"It is too bad that these kids and their parents don't get it. This is about playing basketball and being good sportsmen…sportspeople," he said, looking at Kia.

"Thanks," she said.

"I reffed two of their games in the first round," he said, shaking his head. "They spent less time playing than they did trash talking and trying to intimidate the other teams. Congratulations on making it to the finals."

"So there's only two teams left?" I asked.

"There will be after this round. The other semifinal game is still going on. You four get a break because of the disqualification."

"When is the next game?" I asked.

The ref pulled a schedule out of his pocket and ran a finger down the paper.

"The winner of this semifinal plays at three o'clock." He looked at his watch. "So you have a little more than an hour before the game starts. You have plenty of time."

"And do you know which court we're on?" I asked.

"That's easy. You'll be playing right over there," he said, pointing toward the bleachers.

"The center court?" Ned gasped.

"That's where all the finals are being held," he said. "So good luck."

"Thanks!" Kia answered as the ref walked away.

"Boy...the big center court...that's...that's..."

"Scary," I said, completing his sentence.

"Yeah, scary," he agreed. "Does that sound stupid?"

"Not to me," I said.

"You'll do fine," my father said. "The worst thing is to get all nervous thinking about it. You have too much time between this game and the next to think."

"Maybe the kids should do something to take their minds off the game," Ned's mother suggested. "Maybe something fun."

"What did you have in mind?" I asked.

"We could all get something to drink and then go up in the stands and watch a game. Or maybe look at some more of the displays?"

"That would be good," Kia said.

"You can if you want," I said.

"What do you have in mind?" she asked.

"I'm going to watch the other teams play. I want to see what we're going to be facing."

"Maybe that isn't such a great idea," Kia suggested.

"Maybe not...but..."

"You're right," she agreed. "Let's go over and have a look."

# Chapter Sixteen

We settled in among the other people on the sidelines watching the game.

"Do you know who that is?" I asked Kia.

"I recognized them right away," she said.

One team was made up of four guys we knew from rep basketball. Our team had played them twice last year and lost both games. They were part of a good team and were probably the best four players on that very good team.

"Do you think we have a chance against them?" Kia asked.

"Yeah…right. I wonder what the score is?"

"Eleven to three," a woman standing beside me said.

"That figures, they're killing them," I said.

Just as the words got out of my mouth, they put up a shot and it dropped.

"That makes it twelve to three."

"No, no," the woman said. "That makes it eleven to four."

"You're joking, right?"

"No, the blue team is winning."

I looked at the other team. They were all dressed in identical blue uniforms. They had on the same shorts, socks, shirts, and even their shoes matched. I'd never seen any team that had matching shoes.

"They are pretty good," Kia said.

"You'd expect that," the woman said. "They've already won four of these contests this year."

"What do you mean?" I asked.

"They're an all-star team that travels around from city to city competing in three-on-three tournaments. They've already won in Pittsburgh, Indianapolis, Cincinatti and Montreal, as well as finishing second in Detroit."

"How do you know that?" Kia asked.

"You see the tall one?" the woman asked.

He was hard to miss. He was almost as tall as Ned.

"That's my son."

"He's big," I said.

"Not as big as your center," she said.

Ned wasn't even standing with us. How did she know about him?

"Have you seen us play?" I asked.

"We always scout the opposition," she said. "We watched some of the opening round and all of the other playoff games."

I had a sickening feeling come over me.

"That way we know the strengths and weaknesses of each team so that our boys can play the best game they can," she continued.

The sickening feeling suddenly got much, much worse. If they'd been watching us, they knew that Ned couldn't shoot.

"It's so nice to see a young lady playing," the woman said.

"I always play with boys. It's better competition."

"It's a shame that your fourth player can't play," she continued.

"Yeah, Mark has a—"

"Upset stomach," I said, cutting Kia off. "He may play a lot in the next game."

"Oh…I thought somebody mentioned that he had a sprained ankle and couldn't move."

"He can run if we need him…the ankle was a long time ago…it's healed."

Kia gave me the strangest look but kept her mouth closed.

"And your big man…what's his name?"

"Ned," Kia answered.

"He hasn't played much basketball, has he?"

"A lot. He's played a lot," I answered.

"Oh," she said, sounding like she didn't really believe me. "Your team was very fortunate with that disqualification. You were facing an excellent team. I thought we'd be meeting them in the finals."

Which meant, of course, that she didn't think we would have beat them. That was hard to argue with. I didn't think we could have beaten them either.

I didn't want to answer any more of her questions. She wasn't just making conversation. She was scouting us, or maybe trying to get inside our heads. Either way it was working.

I turned my attention back to the game. It was obvious that both teams were good, but the blue team was better. They rotated players in and out and all four could play. Two were fast and could move the ball. One was an outside shooter, and the big guy stayed under the net. If anything he was the weak link in their team. He was awkward and not that fast, and, while he made a basket, he threw up two bricks before that.

"Game point!" yelled out the scorekeeper.

The ball was back up at the top of the key. The blue team covered their men.

"Break!" called the man.

He fed the ball in and it came right back out to him. He put up a wild three-point shot, which clanked off the backboard. The rebound was gobbled up by the big guy in the blue. He instantly fired it out to one of his players. The ball was no sooner in his hands than it was fed back inside and the big guy deposited it in the net for game.

"Way to go guys!" the woman screamed and clapped her hands for them. She started to walk away, and then stopped, and turned back around. "Good luck!"

"Thanks," I mumbled.

"I think we're in trouble," Kia said.

"Not me. I *know* we're in trouble."

# Chapter Seventeen

"This isn't going to work!" Ned protested.

"It has to," Kia said. "It's our only chance."

"Why don't we just keep doing what we've done in the other games?" he demanded.

"Because it isn't going to work. They've seen us play and they'll defend it."

"Maybe not," Ned said.

"If they don't, then we'll go back to outside shooting, but if they don't cover you—"

"Which is what we think will happen," Kia said, cutting me off.

"Then we have no choice. We'll get you the ball and you're going to have to shoot."

"That guy is big."

"He's not as big as you," I said. "You can do it."

"I'm just not sure."

"Look," I said. "We can start with a play out to Kia or me if you want, but I know they're going to be waiting for that. I know it. Can we just try?"

Ned reluctantly nodded his head in agreement.

"Besides, what have we got to lose?" I asked. "Did anybody think we'd get this far?"

"I did. I thought we could win," Ned said. "I guess I still think we can."

I smiled. "A few good shots, a few lucky bounces, and anything's possible," I said.

"Possible, but not probable, is that what you're saying?" Ned asked.

"We have to be realistic. About the only chance we have is if we can beat them down low."

"You mean if I can beat them down low, right?" Ned asked.

I nodded my head.

***

I looked all around. We were surrounded on three sides by bleachers. They were half-filled—about two hundred people were watching. My dad sat in the front row beside Debbie. Kia was squatted down in front of them. She wasn't starting the game.

"You feeling okay, Ned?" I asked.

"Nope."

"Neither am I. Just remember to—"

"Let's get it started," the ref called out.

"We'll do fine," I said to Ned.

I took the ball up to the top of the court. We had the ball to start because we'd won the coin toss. That might be the only thing we'd win this game.

"Check," I said as I bounced the ball to the man who had come out to cover me.

"Good luck and have a good game," he said as he bounced a pass back to me.

"Um…thanks."

I took one more look around. Here we were, center court, surrounded by hundreds of people, in the finals. Sixteen baskets away from a win. It could happen.

"Break!" I yelled.

Mark hobbled to the side, his man practically glued to him. Ned went to the low post and his man struggled against him, trying to push him away. I shifted to the side and put in a bounce pass to Ned. The ball came to him, bounced slightly away and he reached out and grabbed it.

He faked a pass and then spun around and threw the ball at the hoop. It hit the bottom of the rim, and Ned and their man scrambled after the ball. Somehow Ned got it and threw it up again. It hit the backboard and went in the net!

"It's a basket!" Ned screamed. "A basket!"

I turned around in shock as the audience cheered.

"Ned, go out and cover the throw-in man."

He didn't move. He was frozen, looking up at the crowd.

"Ned!" I screamed and he turned to me.

"Go out and cover the throw-in man. Mark, go under the hoop against the big man."

Both of them looked at me like I was crazy.

"Just do it!" I yelled, and they both scrambled to their positions.

The man tossed the ball to Ned. Ned passed it back to him. Thank goodness he'd remembered it was just a check.

Their player looked around for an open man. I stayed as close as I could to my man, leaving him only one option—throwing it to the man under the hoop. Mark was trying his best to get position, but he couldn't push off on that one foot and was so much smaller to begin with. I knew it was a bad mismatch, but what else could we do? Mark couldn't move enough to cover anybody else.

The ball sailed in, high and toward the net. Their big man grabbed the ball, spun around and shot. It dropped in for an easy basket.

"Sub in," I said to the ref.

Kia came in and Mark went out. The blue team also put in their sub.

The ref tossed me the ball and I walked it out to the top of the court. I passed the ball out to be checked.

"Break!" I yelled.

Kia broke down low, trying to use Ned as a screen. As she ran by, both her man and Ned's man followed after her as she screamed for the pass. I lobbed a soft pass over everybody's head to Ned. He turned around and put up the shot…it missed…he grabbed the rebound to shot and—

"Foul!" the ref yelled out.

He took the ball and tossed it back out to me.

"Buzz!" I called out.

It actually didn't matter what I called. Each play was going to be basically the same—me throwing the ball to Ned and him putting it up—until they starting covering him. If they had been scouting our games the way I thought, they'd been told about some of our plays as well.

Kia scrambled around, trying to get free. She cut in between my man and me and I practically handed her the ball. She dribbled off to the side and threw the ball in to Ned. He hesitated for a split second and then tossed it up. I started to charge in for the rebound and it dropped in!

"Great shot, Ned!" I screamed. "Stay low…stay on their big man!"

Somehow, against all the odds, this was working.

\*\*\*

I moved out and took the check of the ball. The pass went in to Kia's man. She had to take him tight because he was such a good outside shooter. He went to shoot and she jumped up and—he faked the shot and dribbled around her and went up for a lay-up and—*smack!*—Ned reached out and smashed the ball away. I scrambled after it, grabbed the ball and threw it out to Kia, alone on the edge of the line. Her man rushed back out as she threw up a shot and…basket! That counted for two and we were suddenly in the lead 13 to 11.

"Timeout!" called out one of their players. He handed the ball to the ref.

They walked over to their coach as we collected around my father. Ned's mother had looked at all the old scores on the big board and no team had gotten this many points on this team the entire tournament. That was sort of a victory all by itself. But now I didn't want "sort of a victory." I wanted to win.

"I think you have them a little bit scared and a lot confused," my father said.

"They don't know what to expect from us," Kia said. "But neither do I."

That had been our whole strategy the entire game—do whatever wasn't expected. Instead of their scouting working for them it was working for us.

"Maybe it's time," my father said. "What do you think about running some plays the regular way? That's now what they won't expect."

"Do you think it would work?" I asked.

"They're covering Ned tight. A couple of times they've dropped a second man in looking for the rebound," he said. "They're expecting him to shoot."

"Can you fake a shot and then put it outside?" I asked Ned.

"I guess so…I'm really tired."

"So is their center. He's not used to playing the whole game. You're wearing him down too."

"Do you think so?"

"He's dragging. He's been spending a lot of energy trying to push you out. He's not used to playing against somebody who's bigger than he is. Keep pushing back."

"Let's go!" the ref called out.

"First time we get the ball it goes in to Ned for a fake shot and pass back to Kia for the shot. Let's do it."

It was their ball to start after the timeout. I started out to the top of the key to cover the throw-in then I stopped.

"Ned, go out top."

He looked a little thrown by what I'd said, but started out anyway. I went under the hoop against their big man. He wasn't as big as Ned but was a lot bigger than me. I took up a position between him and the ball, leaving him free if they could lob a pass over top of me. I started pushing into him, even before the ball had been checked. He hardly budged. I turned around and with both hands pushed against him, forcing him over and—

"Foul under the net!" the ref yelled out.

"How many is that?" I asked.

"Six. Next foul they shoot."

"Thanks."

The ball was still in the hands of their man, and he

went to check the ball again. Before Ned could even return the ball, I turned around and shoved their center hard with both hands.

"Hey, what are you—"

I shoved him again before he could finish his sentence.

"Another foul under the hoop. Blue team to shoot!"

Kia walked over to me. "What are you doing?" she quietly hissed at me.

"I don't think he can shoot," I whispered back.

He took the ball to the foul line, bounced it twice and shot. It bounced off the rim and missed. It was our ball.

"You made a good guess," Kia said as she brushed by.

"Now let's have a good shot."

I took the ball at the top, quickly checking it.

"Monarch!" I yelled out.

Ned broke down the line to low post and Kia curved around him. His hands were up, but the other center was practically wrapped around him. They were really battling, pushing and shoving each other with their bodies. There was no way I could get the ball inside to him even if I wanted. Kia broke free and I passed it in to her. She dribbled, looking for an opening. I faked one way and then set up a screen for her. She broke around me and lobbed the ball inside to Ned—he'd got position. He faked the shot, drawing in my man.

"Ned!" Kia yelled.

He looked at her, went to throw the pass, but in that instant realized she was covered. He threw it out to me. I aimed and threw it up…spinning, spinning, spinning and in for two points!

"Game point!" the scorekeeper yelled out.

"Timeout!" their coach yelled, and they started off the court.

"Sorry," the scorekeeper said. "You're out of timeouts."

"We can't be!" their coach protested.

"You are," the scorekeeper stated.

The ref picked up the ball. "Play the game," he said as he tossed the ball to one of their men.

"Eleven!" their coach yelled. "Eleven!"

Eleven…I knew that play. Their big man was going to come outside and set a screen for my man who'd get the ball and drive.

"Ned," I said. "Go out and check the ball… slowly."

I walked up to their center under the net. I wanted to foul him again so he'd have to shoot. Instantly I started pushing against him, using my legs, body and arms. He pushed back hard and I couldn't budge him. He shoved back harder and I bounced slightly.

"Eleven!" called out their man.

Instantly their center shifted, running to the top of the key. I stayed down low, waiting. The man rushed by their center, losing Ned. I lunged out as the ball came in and tipped it away, falling forward on my face onto the asphalt. Kia grabbed the ball! We had the ball! I quickly picked myself up and—

"Timeout!" the ref yelled.

I looked around. Who had called a timeout?

"Substitution!" the ref called out.

"Who's changing?" I demanded.

"You."

"Me? Why am I changing?"

"Your face."

"What's wrong with my—" I put a hand up and it stung. I looked at my hand and it was covered in blood.

"We can't let you play until the bleeding stops," the ref said.

"But the game is almost—"

"Sorry," he said, shaking his head. "You've played a good game."

"Come on, Nick," my father said, taking me by the arm and guiding me to the sidelines.

"Maybe we can stop the bleeding and I can go back out," I said.

My father shook his head. "That's not going to happen."

"What is going to happen?" Kia asked.

"You only need a point so it should be something inside," my father said.

"But what?" I asked.

"How about Mark throws it in to Ned and Kia stays up high," my father suggested.

"Then what?" Ned asked.

"Then you put it in the basket," I said.

I expected Ned to argue. Instead he smiled.

"Do you want it straight in or off the backboard?"

"Either way is fine," I said.

They went back out onto the court and I was left to watch. Mark took the check.

"Break!" he yelled loudly.

Wow…Mark yelled…that was amazing in itself.

Without hesitation Mark threw a soft lob pass in to Ned. His man was battling him hard for position, pushing, and Ned tumbled over to the ground!

"Foul on blue!"

Foul! That meant Ned had to shoot a foul shot! He'd never hit a shot from that distance in his entire life.

Mark offered Ned a hand and went to pull him up. Ned was so much bigger that he almost pulled Mark over before getting up.

The ref handed him the ball and he shuffled up to the line.

"Ned!" I called out and he looked over at me. "It doesn't matter. If you miss it or if you make it…it doesn't matter!"

He looked like he didn't believe me. He looked worried. No, worse than worried. He looked scared.

"Just shoot Ned…and don't worry."

Ned bounced the ball. He bounced it again. I turned slightly away, just looking at him out of the corner of my eye. He bounced the ball again, and then as he shot I closed my eyes completely and—

"He made it!" my father screamed. "He made it! He made it!"

# Chapter Eighteen

"Congratulations, good game," their player said as he shook my hand.

"You too, good game," I replied.

"You played great. Hope that doesn't hurt too much," the next player said, pointing to the scrape on my face.

"Thanks…it's okay."

I had to hand it to these guys. They weren't just good players, they were also good sports.

"Well guys, we have to go over to the official's table now," my father said. "That's where you get your trophies."

"We get trophies?" Ned asked.

"Big trophies," Kia said.

"I've never won a trophy before…this is great."

I'd won more than my fair share of trophies over

the years, but this one would be special—more special than any of the others.

"I know exactly where I'm putting mine," Kia said.

"Me too," Mark said. "How about you Ned?"

"I have no idea...I have to think about it."

"Maybe I can help you come up with a place," I suggested.

"You can?" Ned asked.

"Sure. We'll look all around your house until we find the right place."

"Look around my house?" Ned asked.

"You are going to let me look around, aren't you? You know, when I come for my visit. I'm still invited, aren't I?"

"Of course you are...isn't he, Mom?"

"Certainly! We'd love to have Nick come and spend as long as he wants with us!"

"I can go, can't I?" I asked my father.

"That's not a problem. But first things first. Let's go and get your trophies...your championship trophies."

**Eric Walters** lives in Mississauga, Ontario, and spends as much time as possible visiting kids in classrooms all over the country.

# Read all the titles in the Eric Walters basketball series.

**Boot Camp**
*Eric Walters, Jerome Williams &
Johnnie Williams III*
978-1-55143-695-1

**Full Court Press**
*Eric Walters*
978-1-55143-169-7

**Hoop Crazy!**
*Eric Walters*
978-1-55143-184-0

**Long Shot**
*Eric Walters*
978-1-55143-216-8

**Off Season**
*Eric Walters*
978-1-55143-237-3

**Road Trip**
*Eric Walters*
978-1-55143-201-4

**Three on Three**
*Eric Walters*
978-1-55143-170-3

**Triple Threat**
*Eric Walters & Jerome Williams*
978-1-55143-359-2

**Underdog**
*Eric Walters*
978-1-55143-302-8